"Where are you taking me?"

As Jenna told Shane about her favorite place on the planet, she turned in the seat to back the car down the long driveway. Her hand brushed against Shane's shoulder. The sensation set off a zing of awareness that penetrated his body armor of denial like a hollow-point bullet.

Crap.

The first time she'd accidentally bumped into him, he'd attributed his response to having been without sex for so long. But after the X-rated dream he'd had just before dawn… Nope. This was bad news. He was attracted to her. Which completely sucked, since he'd just talked Jenna into working with him for the coming week.

Script. Focus. The words sounded good, familiar—comforting, even.

"The view is very nice," Jenna was saying. "And nobody goes to the spot where I'm taking you."

Alone. In the woods. On a beautiful morning with the woman of his dreams.

The same woman who would carve his heart out of his chest with a dull spoon if she knew what he knew…

Dear Reader,

Welcome to Sentinel Pass! When the idea for this series first started to germinate in my mind, I knew two things: I wanted to set it in the Black Hills of South Dakota and I wanted my heroines to belong to a book club. Why? Because I have fond memories of living in the Hills as a young mother, and because I am currently a member of a book club that replenishes my life in innumerable ways. Libby, Jenna, Kat and Char are lucky to have each other—especially when certain men arrive to upset the status quo.

Jenna Murphy isn't a fan of change—there's safety in routine. But suddenly Hollywood's spotlight is trained directly on her little world and Sentinel Pass is being overrun with strangers who plan to make a television show called *Sentinel Passtime*. One of the first to appear is the show's handsome, enigmatic producer, Shane Reynard...who seems familiar.

Shane's droll sense of humor and unfaltering support of his best friend in *Baby By Contract* told me he'd make a great hero. And when fate provides him with the chance to make something good happen in Jenna Murphy's life, he doesn't hesitate to act—even knowing he might lose his heart to a woman who has every right to hate him.

For insider information on what's happening in Sentinel Pass, please visit my Web site, www.debrasalonen.com. Or write me at P.O. Box 322, Cathey's Valley, CA 95306.

Happy reading,

Debra Salonen

HIS BROTHER'S SECRET
Debra Salonen

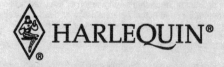

HARLEQUIN®

TORONTO • NEW YORK • LONDON
AMSTERDAM • PARIS • SYDNEY • HAMBURG
STOCKHOLM • ATHENS • TOKYO • MILAN • MADRID
PRAGUE • WARSAW • BUDAPEST • AUCKLAND

ISBN-13: 978-0-373-71516-9
ISBN-10:   0-373-71516-1

HIS BROTHER'S SECRET

www.eHarlequin.com

Printed in U.S.A.

ABOUT THE AUTHOR

Debra has always been an avid and eclectic reader, but her first love was romance. For years, she plotted ways to get one of the Hardy boys to fall in love with Nancy Drew. Belonging to a book club has broadened her reading horizons and many of the titles coincide with what members of the Wine, Women and Words group are reading in the Sentinel Pass series, but she's proud to say her book club friends always include her latest release in their monthly selections—and they give her great reviews. What are friends for?

Books by Debra Salonen

HARLEQUIN SUPERROMANCE
1003—SOMETHING ABOUT EVE
1061—WONDERS NEVER CEASE
1098—MY HUSBAND, MY BABIES
1104—WITHOUT A PAST
1110—THE COMEBACK GIRL
1196—A COWBOY SUMMER
1238—CALEB'S CHRISTMAS WISH
1279—HIS REAL FATHER
1386—A BABY ON THE WAY
1392—WHO NEEDS CUPID?
    "The Max Factor"
1434—LOVE, BY GEORGE
1452—BETTING ON SANTA*
1492—BABY BY CONTRACT†

SIGNATURE SELECT SAGA
BETTING ON GRACE

HARLEQUIN AMERICAN ROMANCE
1114—ONE DADDY TOO MANY
1126—BRINGING BABY HOME
1139—THE QUIET CHILD

*Texas Hold 'Em
†Spotlight on Sentinel Pass

To Donna, Kori, Jan and Heather—good food,
excellent wine and interesting books
make for a fabulous excuse to get together, no?
Thanks for all that you add to my life…
and to my books. Including, but not limited to,
a Bernese mountain dog named Duke.

CHAPTER ONE

"COOPER WANTS TO MARRY ME, Jenna. Can you believe it?"

Libby's voice came across the phone line sounding close to tears and mystified. But Jenna Murphy didn't doubt for a minute that Lib's dreams were about to come true. Nobody deserved this shot at happiness more than Libby McGannon, Sentinel Pass postmaster and Jenna's best friend for more years than either cared to count.

"Me," Libby repeated, before Jenna could respond. "And he asked before I told him about the baby. I think. Wait. Maybe not… Oh, I don't know. My mind is such a swirl of hormones and guilt and worry. But this feels right. Doesn't it? I said yes, anyway. Oh, I've gotta run. He just went to Mac's to formally ask for my hand—isn't that sweet?—but I can see him coming back. Thanks for listening. I love you. Bye."

Jenna slowly replaced the phone on its hook. The Murphy family's phone was an old-fashioned model. Practically museum quality. Black, because black was cheaper. She was proud that her hand didn't shake, not even a little. Surprises had never been her friend. Even good ones took time to become familiar, and thus…safe.

"That was Libby," she told her mother who'd probably been able to hear bits and pieces of Libby's exuberant monologue from where she sat across the room. "Cooper proposed." She swallowed the metallic taste in her mouth. "And Lib said yes."

"Oh, my," Bess Murphy exclaimed, springing up from the kitchen table where mother and daughter had been eating breakfast. Granola and soy milk. Bess's latest health fad. "I knew it. I knew he was in love with her. I could see it in his eyes last night at the town meeting. Even when he was talking about what was going to happen and how the town would benefit from the television production crew coming, he kept looking at Libby. Like a starving man in a 7-Eleven."

Jenna couldn't help but smile at the metaphor. Cooper Lindstrom, TV star and talent show personality, didn't strike her as the type to frequent quick-stop convenience stores. But Bess was renowned for saying the first thing that came into her head—often at her daughter's expense.

"Have they set a date?"

"She didn't mention one, but I imagine it'll be soon," she said, gathering up both empty bowls to put in the bottom rack of the dishwasher. If she left them for her mother to tend to, they might still be on the table when Jenna returned from work. The completion of household chores was dependent on the intensity of one or all of Bess's ailments: arthritis, diabetes, gastro-intestinal troubles, migraines or any other unexplained medical symptom that might flare up, leaving Bess prone on the couch watching *Lifetime* or *Turner Classic Movies*—or, God forbid, *Discovery Health*—for the entire day.

Her mother was a hypochondriac, plain and simple. She'd always been overly wrapped up in everyday aches and pains, but since Jenna's father's death two years earlier,

Bess had honed the art of fretting about her health to a doctorial level.

Bess refilled her coffee mug and leaned casually against the dated, olive-green Formica countertop. "Why do you say that? They haven't known each other long. And Libby was pretty upset with him when she found out Cooper had been playing her for a fool."

Jenna felt her cheeks heat up. She was one of the few people who knew that Libby was pregnant. She'd just assumed that Libby and Cooper would want to make their relationship official before the baby came, but that wasn't always the case these days. "I don't think Lib will hold that against him, Mom. I've known her a long time, and this is the first time I've ever seen her throw caution to the wind—relationshipwise. That says a lot, don't you think?"

Bess didn't answer right away, but at least she seemed distracted from Jenna's gaff. The break in conversation gave Jenna time to pack a small lunch. Apple. Cheese stick. Cookies—the not-so-healthy brand her mother refused to buy. At times, Jenna felt like a child living with her mommy. But most days she felt old. Very old. Caught in a one-sided generational squeeze caring for her ailing mother without the benefit of a husband and family of her own to balance things out.

By choice, she reminded herself. She'd had a couple of chances to unknot the apron strings over the years, but the men she'd dated had been either too much or not enough like her father. Or, in Brian's case, too much like her mother. She honestly had no expectations of ever finding Mr. Right for more reasons than she cared to list—the most verbal of them was looking deep in thought at the moment.

"I'm not surprised Libby fell for Coop. He's like a big, handsomely groomed golden retriever. You just want to hug and pet him. But that friend he brought with him to the meeting wasn't too shabby, either. At first, I thought he was purebred Doberman…because he was dressed all in black, I suppose. But when I looked closer I could see the depth in his eyes. So, I'm calling him Mr. Bernese Mountain Dog."

Jenna shook her head as she rolled the top of her brown paper sack in a neat crease and stapled it. "I'm sure he'd be thrilled to know you think of him as a big slobbery pooch."

"Not just any old dog, dear. My favorite breed. When I was a young girl, our neighbor had one. His name was Franz. His owner went all the way to Switzerland to buy him. Now there are breeders around the country. I always wanted one, but Clarence claimed an animal that size would eat us out of house and home. He'd never budge—even when I played the Jenna card."

"The what?"

"You know how much your dad doted on you. I told him every little girl should have a dog." She pursed her lips and frowned in a way that made her look older than fifty-one. The frumpy cotton housecoat worn over faded pastel blue pajamas and open-toe scuffs didn't help. Jenna remembered a time when her mother looked glamourous and exotic—even before nine in the morning.

She made a mental note to ask the doctor about clinical depression the next time she accompanied her mother to an appointment.

"Clarence said if you wanted a dog that bad, you could buy one when you were paying the bills."

of math math math

Jenna smiled. That sounded like her father. It also reminded her of a debate that Libby had mentioned between her brother, Mac, and his daughter, Megan. The widower had yet to give in on the dog front, but Jenna knew it was only a matter of time. Despite his gruff outward demeanor, Mac was a big softy deep down. Jenna had had a crush on him, off and on, for years. He might actually be the only man she'd consider marrying. Unfortunately, he'd never shown the slightest interest in her, except as his sister's friend.

With a sigh she'd meant to keep silent, Jenna stuffed the lunch sack into her backpack and looked around to see if she was forgetting anything. As usual, she'd laid out things the night before. She double-checked her list just to be sure.

"I know I told you this, Mom, but it's important so please don't call me in an hour asking me to run to Rapid with you," she said walking close enough to make eye contact. "The Health Department is supposed to send out an inspector today. He has to check the new pipes before we can cover up the open trenches. We can't afford to lose another day, otherwise I would have been covering for Libby at the post office."

Her mother's still-pretty lips pursed expressively. "Who'd they get to fill in? Not the girl from Hill City, I hope. Last time she worked I wound up with Rufus Miller's mail." When she shook her head, a lock of silvery blond hair escaped from the knot she'd piled on top of her head. "Libby's excellent, of course, but I miss the way things were when Mary was postmistress."

Libby's grandmother had practically run the town for as long as Jenna could remember. Now in retirement, Mary "lived in sin" with her companion, Calvin. "I know, Mom, but Mary's not doing too well right now. Lib said they had a scary episode yesterday. Calvin's hoping it was just a reaction to a new medication, but they don't know for sure."

Mom sighed heavily. "If I ever start showing signs of dementia, I want you to toss a hair dryer in the water while I'm in the tub."

Jenna had been hearing various exit strategies for the past couple of months. "With my luck, you'd catch it, then accuse me of attempted murder."

"I won't. I promise."

"Dementia robs you of short-term memory, Mom. You might forget that the plan was your idea. Libby's grandmother didn't even recognize her yesterday."

Mom lifted the cup to her lips but didn't drink from it. Instead, she frowned and said, "Well, I'm sure that no matter how bad I get, I'll still know when it's time to exit stage left with grace and flair."

Jenna knew better than to argue. They'd had this discussion as recently as a week ago when her mom thought she'd developed COPD—chronic obstructive pulmonary disease. No one adored diseases that came with abbreviated names more than Bess Murphy. Her doctor had insisted the symptoms were that of a cold. Possibly a little bronchitis. Mom had been crushed.

Her mother needed to get out more. At the very least, she'd benefit from a hobby.

Jenna and her friends in the Wine, Women and Words book club had discussed the topic at length. They'd even invited Bess to join the group. Mom had declined, claiming her failing eyesight was proof of macular degeneration. For some reason, Bess was convinced that her life was on a slippery slope and she could swoosh off into the ethers to join her deceased husband at any moment. A drama queen on skis.

"I probably won't be home until four or five," Jenna said, heading for the door. "You're in charge of supper."

"You're not going to miss *Jeopardy,* are you? Alex Trebek is so cute…in a miniature schnauzer kind of way."

Jenna stopped abruptly and wheeled about. "Mother, what is it with you and dogs? Are you trying to tell me something? Do you want a pet?"

Bess put a hand to her chest as if aghast. "Heavens, no. With all my health problems? What would happen to the poor thing if we bonded, then I died? I wouldn't inflict that kind of anxiety on any living creature. No…no…" She shuffled to the chair she'd vacated earlier and sat. "I…well, if you must know, I've been trying to come up with a character I could play in the new TV show. Say…a quirky older woman who runs a pet adoption service."

Jenna's stomach crimped. She loved her mother. The last thing Jenna wanted was to see her disappointed. She was too emotionally fragile to handle rejection. And Bess's acting experience had been limited to local stages. Surely the people who were turning Libby's story into a television sitcom had a script—and characters—in mind.

"Oh, don't say anything. I can see in your face you think I'm slightly whacko for thinking such a thing, but I've given this a lot of thought, Jenna Mae. Hollywood coming to Sentinel Pass doesn't have to be a bad thing. Not only will the increased traffic and advertising the filming brings in be good for business, but from what Cooper said last night, he and his producer friend are looking for locals to appear in the show."

His tall, dark and handsome producer friend. The Bernese mountain dog. The guy who had set off all kinds of weird bells and whistles the moment he walked into Char's gift shop where Jenna had been working yesterday afternoon. The man who'd disappeared like a ghost a short while later.

Jenna made herself focus on her mother. Dreams were good—to a degree. But the chance of Bess securing even a bit part in some not-yet-written TV show seemed pretty iffy. And Jenna knew who would be left to pick up the pieces when nothing came of all this dog talk. "I'm sure Cooper means well, Mom, but the only way the Mystery Spot is going to benefit is if we're open for business. Have you thought any more about your hours this summer?"

Jenna and Bess had been having this discussion for weeks—no, months. Bess made a limp, noncommittal gesture. "I really don't know if I'm up to it this year, Jenna. The arthritis in my back isn't helped by standing around taking tickets and playing tour guide to a bunch of tourists."

"What arthritis?" Jenna almost asked. So far, not one of her mother's many X-rays had shown even a hint of arthritic deposits.

"Well, you know our budget as well as I do, Mom. If I have to hire someone to take your place, there won't be any money left for the improvements we have slated. Like paving the parking lot."

All vibrancy left her mother's face, making Jenna regret her impatient tone. She could blame her short temper on budget woes, but those were ever present in a small, tourist-oriented business. The real cause was something she didn't want to talk about. Or think about. Her chase dream had returned last night. An old, unwelcome *friend* that had been a constant in her life through most of her twenties. It always started with a pleasant, harmless stroll down a busy street but ended in a heart-racing pursuit by a faceless demon whose heavy breathing reminded her vividly of a memory she thought she'd mastered.

"Sorry," she said, crossing to the chair where her mother sat. She gave her a hug, gently patting her back as she might a child. "I'm just a little tense because it's the middle of June and we're not open. I probably should have hired someone else to fix the broken water line, but I felt so sorry for Walt."

Walt Gruen was the plumbing contractor she'd hired to repair her broken water line. Unfortunately, his college-age daughter had been injured in a car accident a few days after he started the job and he'd had to drop everything to attend to her in Denver. Since he worked alone—for a fee even Jenna could afford—there was no one to pick up the slack.

"I know, dear. But you can't blame yourself. This kind of thing was bound to happen. I warned your father about taking shortcuts, but you know how he was with money." Bess shook her head. She was one of the special women who gray with such grace and beauty it would be a sacrilege to color her hair. Jenna feared she wasn't going to be that lucky since she'd inherited her father's red hair.

Clarence Murphy had been sixty-four when he suffered a heart attack one morning before leaving for school. Scientist, teacher and mastermind behind the popular summer attraction that had baffled and intrigued visitors for twenty-odd years, his death had been mourned by many. Jenna had been a part of the family's summer business almost from its inception, but her father had sheltered her from one undeniable truth: her mother couldn't be trusted with money. His widely reputed miserliness may have been prompted by a need to offset his wife's tendency to spend without reservation. Every day, Jenna felt she understood her father better.

"I know that's what you think, Mom, but I can't figure out why the break happened so long *after* the frost melted." Jenna sighed. They'd been over this ground before. The pipe broke and needed to be fixed before they could reopen. Bottom line. "I'd better go. Don't want to miss the inspector. I'm just sorry I didn't schedule this for yesterday. Then I could have subbed for Libby today instead of holding down the fort for Char. The post office pays better."

"But if you hadn't been working at the teepee, you wouldn't have met Mr. Bernese Mountain Dog." Her mother fluttered her eyelashes coquettishly. "Tell me again what he said."

Jenna paused, hand on the doorknob. She'd never understood her mother's fascination with Hollywood. Bess had nearly wet herself the first time she heard Cooper Lindstrom was in town, and last night when introduced to a real live producer, she'd gotten honest-to-goodness stars in her eyes.

"His name is Shane something. I only remember that because I knew a guy in college named Shane. Not knewknew, but we had a class together. And, to be honest, this Shane didn't leave that much of an impression." *Liar*. "We barely exchanged two words before Coop showed up asking where he stood with Libby. Your Bernese mountain dog slipped away."

Bess looked in the direction of the McGannon homes. "And now Libby is getting married. There's hope for you, yet, honey."

Jenna didn't see the correlation, but she let the comment pass. She was happy for her friend, who, with a little luck, might get some well-deserved happiness—*and* the baby she'd gone to such extreme lengths to procure. "Gotta go, Mom. Bye," she mumbled.

"Wait. Promise me one thing."

Jenna held her sigh as she paused in the doorway. "What?"

"If you bump into the handsome producer, try not to mutter. It's distracting and makes you appear a little odd."

"What on earth makes you think I'll be seeing him? He and Coop are supposed to be holding open meetings for the townsfolk this week. I'm going to be busy at the Mystery Spot trying to get the plumbing fixed so we can open and start earning enough money to pay our taxes."

Her mother's reply was one Jenna had heard a million times. "I just have a feeling. You'll see."

As always, Jenna wished she'd been born with a bit less of her father's pragmatism and a bit more of her mother's optimism. Maybe then she wouldn't spend all of her time worrying.

SHIMMERING LINES BOUNCE off hot pavement.
Wavy, unbalanced. Like a girl
Going nowhere.
Fast.

"'Going nowhere fast,'" Shane repeated, as he looked up from the small volume of poetry that Coop had given him.

Kinda like me yesterday.

He shook his head, still embarrassed by the way he'd reacted to seeing Jenna behind the counter of the big teepee: like an inexperienced schoolboy drooling over the girl of his dreams. He'd come to South Dakota to find her, he just hadn't expected her to be the first person he bumped into.

And he hadn't expected her to be so vivid. Possibly more beautiful than he remembered. Definitely more real than the tragic figure he'd made her into in his mind.

He pushed the heel of his hand against the uncomfortable pressure behind his breastbone and shifted in the car seat. He didn't know why he'd never been able to get Jenna Murphy out of his head, but she'd definitely been part of his motivation for joining Cooper in Sentinel Pass.

If he could work up the nerve to contact her.

He reached around the steering column to turn the key in the ignition. The Cadillac's dashboard lit up impressively, giving him the pertinent facts of time and outside temperature. He lowered the driver's-side window a few inches and took in a deep breath of dewy, pine-scented air.

He'd been sitting in this car in front of Libby McGannon's house for over an hour after dropping off Cooper. Not because he lacked a plan—Coop had set the ball in motion the night before and people were expecting them to show up at the local restaurant—but Shane knew he'd be worthless until he got this thing with Jenna off his chest. Something he could have done yesterday but didn't.

He sighed and slumped down in the wide, comfortable leather seat. Maybe if he'd been better prepared. Had some kind of dialogue scripted in his head. But what do you say to the girl whose life you ruined?

Hi, Jenna. Remember me? Shane from art appreciation class. College. The semester you were raped.

He groaned and wiped his sweaty palms on his trademark black jeans. What the hell was wrong with him? He wasn't a kid who didn't have a clue about what he wanted to do with his life. He was a successful television producer, director and screenwriter. He'd made a lot of money at a profession he enjoyed and was good at. His shelf full of awards—including an Oscar for his adaptation of a popular novel a few years back—was nothing to sneeze at, as his mother might have said. She would have been proud of him. And happy for him. Although he knew his personal life—or lack of one—would have concerned her.

But she'd been gone nearly six years. Six years that had weighed heavily on Shane since her deathbed confession of a secret that probably had shortened her life through the suffocating effects of the guilt. Shane also blamed that secret in no small part for the state of his love life.

He'd lost count of the times he'd drowned his sorrows in a bottle of scotch, wishing for the impossible. That Mom had taken her secret to her grave. Or, even better, that he'd been born an only child.

Unfortunately, Shane had only to look in the mirror to be reminded of his brother. Adam. His identical twin. His opposite in every way that counted, though. Or so Shane hoped.

There were some in Hollywood who called Shane "the monk" behind his back. He often made the club scene but usually alone, unless work was involved. He dated on occasion but seldom took out the same woman twice. Luckily, he lived in a place and time where women enjoyed sex for the same reasons men did and weren't necessarily looking for a long-term attachment.

If that made his life seem shallow and superficial, he didn't really care. He couldn't name a single person he was trying to impress. He'd cut all ties with Adam after their mother's funeral. He'd done the same with his father a few months later when the old man married a woman half his age. His father's act merely confirmed what Shane had always known about his dysfunctional family—the nucleus was split evenly down the middle. He and his mother on one side. Adam and their father on the other. The gulf between the two factions was wide and deep. And Shane hoped it would stay that way. For Jenna Murphy's sake.

He closed the book and studied it. *Ashes of Hope* by Jenna M. Murphy. Deep maroon watermarked silk with gold leaf lettering. Elegant and ladylike. A little old-fashioned given the age of the author, he thought, but serene. Perhaps to mitigate the austerity of the poems, which, from the dozen or so he'd read, were intense, deeply personal and poignant.

Coop had given him the self-published treatise as a bribe to get Shane to confess how he knew Jenna, who was Libby McGannon's best friend. Libby, the catalyst who had set this whole, unwieldy circus in motion.

Shane hadn't intended to blurt out the fact that he recognized Jenna, but seeing her behind the counter of the teepee-shaped gift shop minutes after arriving in Sentinel Pass had left him badly shaken up. And naturally that kind of only-in-the-movies coincidence sparked Coop's curiosity. What Coop didn't know—and Shane had no intention of sharing—was the fact that Jenna was Shane's sole purpose for being in the Black Hills.

He could have delegated the research part of this trip to any one of a dozen minions. But from Coop's very first mention of an online ad offering part ownership in a working gold mine in Sentinel Pass, South Dakota, Shane had known his past had finally caught up with him. There simply was no other explanation. Fate? God? Karma? Shane didn't believe in any of them. But he firmly believed every person was capable of manifesting his or her own reality. For the past six years, Shane's reality had included the ethereal image of a young woman he'd barely known for one short semester in his senior year of college. She haunted him at night. Not the happy, exuberant persona that had attracted him in the first place, but the hollow-eyed ghost of a girl in the backseat of her parents' car as they took her home weeks before the normally scheduled holiday break. As far as he knew, she never returned to campus.

That girl was the reason he was here.

His plan—if you could call it that—was to ease his conscience and, if possible, to make amends.

Still, did she have to be the first person he saw? But there she'd been—that red hair a dead giveaway. Behind a counter filled with Native American jewelry.

She hadn't recognized him. A fact that didn't surprise him, given how much he'd changed since college. He was a different person, really. Short hair. A new name. LASIK surgery to lose the coke-bottle-bottom glasses.

But *she* was every bit as beautiful as he remembered…with a few changes. Her gorgeous red hair was shoulder length instead of all the way to her waist. Now she was the one with glasses. Small, stylish black frames drew attention to her flashing green-gold eyes, alive with wit and wisdom. She'd laughed a lot back then. Until the night she attended a party and became the victim of something the news media had branded the date-rape drug. Her attacker was never caught.

Shane heaved a weighty sigh and reached for the thermal travel mug he'd purchased that morning. He polished off the last gulp. Cold, but to his profound surprise, the brew wasn't bad—unlike what his mother had passed off as coffee when he'd been growing up in Minnesota.

In atypical Coop fashion, his friend had rousted Shane at the break of dawn to drive him to the local bakery to buy doughnuts and jelly rolls, which he planned to use as props when he proposed to Libby.

Shane set the container back in the cup holder and leaned forward to rest his arms on the steering wheel. He wondered how it was going for his friend inside the unpretentious two-story home. There was no outward sign of life, but a dark-haired man—Libby's brother, Shane was pretty sure—had come and gone on foot half an hour earlier.

There hadn't been any gunshots. Shane had been listening. Sorta. Mostly, he'd read the words of Jenna's poetry, trying to catch a glimpse of the girl he'd fallen in love with. Well, he'd called what he'd felt *love*. Maybe it was infatuation. Lord knew it was one-sided, completely unrequited. He and Jenna hadn't exchanged more than a dozen words that semester, but that didn't stop his knees from getting weak whenever he saw her walking across campus.

He closed his eyes and smiled. Walking didn't come close to describing the way Jenna Murphy moved. She danced with barely contained energy, like a happy hummingbird. The first time he saw her he'd assumed she was a theater major because she moved like a dancer and her voice carried as if she'd been trained to project. But he came to realize that was her "tour guide" voice. A by-product of spending her summers working in her parents' business—a Sentinel Pass tourist trap called the Mystery Spot.

He'd spent hours constructing elaborate daydreams about visiting her at the place. Although that was before Jenna was attacked and left school. Before he dropped out and moved to California. He hadn't been back to South Dakota since. Until now.

According to Coop's plan that he'd laid out at the town meeting the night before, Shane was supposed to be "mingling with the locals."

"Starting, perhaps, with the redhead who made the usually glib and suave Shane Reynard turn into a stammering schoolboy," his friend had added, poking Shane with his bony elbow before hopping out the car.

Coop had even provided a crudely sketched map to find the Mystery Spot.

"I heard all about the place from Jenna's mother, Bess, when I was here before," Coop had told him. "Apparently, Jenna's dad was some kind of eccentric college professor with a passion for optical illusions, although everyone pretends the exhibits are part of some scientific anomaly. I didn't actually set foot inside, but it sounds like a hoot."

Shane picked up the oversize sticky note that was attached to the passenger seat and studied the purple felt-tip marker scribbles. The funny jittery sensation under his rib cage started again. Too much caffeine, he figured.

Or was it from knowing he was about to reconnect with Jenna?

"I know you said she didn't remember you from college," Coop had said before turning in last night, "but I bet she would if you introduced yourself using your family name. That might jog her memory."

Shane didn't doubt that for a minute. After all, it was the name of the man who raped her.

CHAPTER TWO

AS HE FOLLOWED Cooper's map, Shane kept one part of his brain on the alert for possible background locations. Production was still weeks off—awaiting a viable script and cast. Coop, the project's coproducer, had promised to help write the pilot once he had his personal life back on track.

For the first time in his life, Shane felt a niggling hint of sympathy for Coop's late mom, Lena. The woman had had final say on Coop's career and ran his life as if she were the CEO of it. Lena and Shane had butted heads many times, but he could see how trying it must have been keeping her exuberant, attention-challenged son on task.

And, in a way, Lena's death was partly behind Shane's decision to come here. Helping Coop deal with the loss had stirred up all the feelings—love, hate, guilt and regret— Shane had spent six years trying to master after his own mother died.

At Main Street, he turned right and was relieved to see a billboard promoting the Mystery Spot. The brilliant yellow zigzag lines against a vivid purple background were almost enough to make a person dizzy.

"Nice." He leaned across the seat to take a photo.

The signs got bigger and more elaborate the closer he got to his destination.

Only Two Miles To The Thrill Of A lifetime.

Just One More Mile To A Mind-Blowing Experience.

Three Hundred Feet To The M Spot.

That one made him grin.

Maybe he could work this place into the script. Offer Jenna some ridiculous amount to rent the facility when they started filming. She wouldn't know the going rate so he could be as generous as he wanted. Needed.

What is *the going rate for conscience absolution these days?*

He stepped on the gas to make the car climb an incline but had to slam on the brakes a few seconds later. A pair of orange plastic hazard cones blocked his entrance into the Mystery Spot's gravel parking lot. He leaned forward to read the hand-written notes attached to the markers.

On the left was: Closed For Repairs… Sorry. The right one read: Really. We Are. Please Come Again.

He somehow knew the sentiments belonged to Jenna. And he believed her. Maybe because of the sad face under *Sorry.* Coop hadn't mentioned any kind of problems at the place so whatever the issue it must have come up after Cooper left town.

Feeling both disappointed and slightly relieved, Shane pulled close enough to the cones so his Escalade was off the road, then he put the car in Park. Big lot, he thought, looking around. They must do a lot of business.

But clumps of weeds poking through the gravel base gave the impression the site hadn't seen much traffic lately. Plus, the lack of surfacing without lines to delineate parking spaces made it look like a giant door ding waiting to happen.

Across the two-block expanse was a gigantic purple-and-yellow arrow attached to an eight-foot-high wooden fence that managed to obscure any view of the buildings behind it. He could make out four or five roofs of varying sizes and shapes nestled at the base of a stand of pines marching up the hillside.

The Mystery Spot would remain a mystery a bit longer, he thought, picking up his digital Nikon. Studying the large LED screen on the back, he hit the zoom toggle and brought the front gate into focus.

A flash of movement near the far corner of the fence line made him swing it to the left. Was that a person?

He clicked a shot without thinking then lowered the camera, leaned forward and squinted. Yes. Someone was prowling around the fence.

It could be anybody, he told himself. Probably an employee. *But the place is closed. And there aren't any cars in the parking lot.*

He opened the door and got out to stand on the SUV's running board, where he had an unobstructed view of the place. It was still early, but the sun had risen into a cloud-free sky. The bright morning light reflecting off the pale gravel made his eyes water. He was just bending down for his sunglasses when he heard the unmistakable sound of glass breaking.

"Oh, crap," he muttered.

He hopped to the ground and kicked aside the "Sorry" cone to allow the vehicle in the lot before climbing behind the wheel again.

The smart thing to do was to call the cops. But he had an L.A.-dweller's aversion to police involvement. And he didn't even know if Sentinel Pass had a police force. By the time the state patrol or highway cops got here, the place could be robbed blind.

Instead of roaring across the open lot, he circumnavigated the perimeter, which put him close to the place where he'd seen the movement. He stayed in the car, scoping out the area. The main entrance, which was secured by a thick chain and padlock, was about a hundred feet ahead. The fence made a perpendicular turn and disappeared into the trees and out of sight, encircling the whole compound, he assumed.

He got out of the car, taking his phone with him. *Maybe there's a back entrance,* he thought, pocketing his keys. *There's probably an employee parking lot that I can't see and I'm going to look stupid when—*

"Shit."

About ten feet ahead—where the fence started to curve making it not easily spotted from the parking lot—two boards had been pried off and cast aside. Big rusty nails pointed upward. That definitely wasn't the work of an employee. The opening wasn't huge, but he could squeeze through if he wanted to try.

Don't even think about it, he silently cautioned over the loud thudding in his ears.

But a creaking sound from inside the compound made him slip between the rough planks and flatten his back against the fence. He looked around. Only the back side of one rustic log cabin was visible. No windows had been cut into the dark brown-stained wood. The building was taller than a normal house thanks to the three-foot-tall rock and mortar foundation.

Overgrown grass and weeds, still glistening with dew, showed the path someone had taken recently. The trail went around the far side of the building.

Feeling both silly and nervous, he sidestepped along the fence until he could see around the corner of the cabin.

Nothing. Nobody. Just a more complete view of the layout. A center courtyard that featured an obelisk of some kind under a gazebo with a pyramid-shaped roof. He'd seen the top of that from outside and wondered about it.

Sidewalks radiated outward from that hub like spokes on a wheel, but the paths were wiggly, like the signs he'd seen.

He took a deep breath and slowly walked toward the main hub, sticking close to the building. His mouth was dry and he wished he'd turned around when he'd had the chance, but now his curiosity was aroused.

Unfortunately, curiosity had been his biggest downfall where his brother was concerned. Adam had sucked Shane into one brutal joke after another. Like the time they played Lone Ranger, and Adam tied Shane to the clothesline post in their St. Paul backyard—and left him there.

"Why are you so gullible, Shane?" their father had asked several hours later when he and Mom returned home from some function.

His mom had rushed to Shane's aid. "Not gullible. Trusting. Like me. There's a difference."

His father had chuckled. "Maybe this time he'll learn."

"Not if he winds up with pneumonia. Adam needs to be punished for this cruelty. And that blond bimbo baby-sitter fired."

Without warning, his father roughly yanked Shane out of his mother's grasp and made him stand up and face him. Shane remembered shivering uncontrollably because he'd had to pee so badly he'd finally relieved himself and the wet fabric had frozen to his leg. "Learn from this, son, or you'll be the one punished," his father had said sternly. "Do you understand me?"

Shane had. He'd learned never to trust his brother. But fortunately, neither of his parents had been able to squelch his curiosity.

He took another step forward. At least this time, he told himself, his brother wasn't around to make him regret the impulse.

"WHAT THE HECK?"

Jenna braked her bicycle beside the one remaining upright orange cone she'd erected between the curbs. She'd felt horrible about turning away people who had driven all this distance.

Her rear tire skidded slightly and she had to put her foot down to keep her balance. The other cone was lying on its side a few feet away. All she could see of her handmade sign was the sad face, which she'd drawn in black permanent marker.

Her gaze followed the tire tracks that had left a clear trail in the fine dirt that encircled her parking lot, finally settling on a large white SUV parked near the corner of the fence—a strange place to park considering the lot was empty and he could have pulled right up to the main gate.

She didn't recognize the vehicle, but she had a sneaking suspicion she knew its owner. One or both of the Californians who had arrived in town yesterday just in time to participate in the town meeting the night before.

"Oh, for heaven's sake, Cooper," she muttered. "If you wanted to see the place, all you had to do was ask." The nervous flutter in the pit of her stomach evened out—until she realized Coop's friend might be with him, too.

She held on tight to the rubber handgrips as she pedaled across the lot. The gravel beneath her front wheel tested her endurance and balance. She'd hoped to pave the lot this year. At the rate they were going, however, that was a pipe dream.

No pun intended. Their busted pipe that supplied water to the entire property was probably going to wind up costing them a fortune. Two prime weeks of vacation travelers, at the very least. The future revenue from word-of-mouth referrals and repeat business couldn't be counted.

It wasn't easy keeping a small, seasonal business going. If you weren't sweating property taxes and the price of gas, you had to deal with new regulations. Last year they'd been required to add a handicap-approved bathroom, and she was still waiting to find out if her father's artsy, but unevenly paved, paths between buildings had to be changed. Her father would have hated that.

She slowed as she neared the car.

A Cadillac with South Dakota plates, but something about it cried rental. She couldn't say why but she was sure it belonged to Coop and his handsome, mysteriously somber pal. Who, despite what her mother said, was no dog.

Grinning, she hopped off her bike and walked it to the fence. Had Cooper and his friend decided they couldn't wait for a tour and circumnavigated the outside on foot? That was a waste of time. The eight-foot-tall fence only had one entrance—her father's ploy to build on the mystery theme by supposedly protecting the spot's cosmic secrets from prying eyes. Although, if someone broke in, other than the maze, there wasn't anything to see without going into the buildings.

She was about to return to the SUV to look inside when she noticed two boards on the ground. She walked a little closer and saw they'd been pulled from the fence. Her heart rate sped up. Vandals?

Maybe the car didn't belong to Cooper.

She grabbed her bike and quickly wheeled it to the front gate where she soundlessly unlocked the thick chain. The gate was designed to slide sideways along a six-foot-length of track. She only opened it wide enough to slip in, but she didn't bother closing it.

Looking around, she hesitated. Everything looked just as she'd left it. *Maybe Walt's back from Denver.* She discarded the thought. Walt's truck would have been parked out front if he were there to work.

Whoever was in here wasn't a friend. But why would anybody break in? There was nothing of value to steal. A few cheap Mystery Spot trinkets and mementos in the gift shop, maybe. She hadn't even bothered to restock the sodas in the vending machine. Why waste the electricity until she knew for sure they'd be reopening?

She tried to listen for something out of the ordinary, but a squabble amongst crows in the trees made it impossible for her to hear any voices. A shiver passed down her back as it hit her that she was alone at a remote site and her mother wouldn't miss her until much later in the day.

She fingered the skeleton key in her pocket and hurried to the office—a small lean-to that had been a shed in a former life. Her father had spent money where needed on keeping up the exhibits, but his wife and daughter, who handled the paperwork, had been expected to make do.

The door creaked when she opened it. She hurried inside and locked it behind her. Heart pounding, she grabbed the portable phone—the modern, two-receiver unit she'd purchased after her father died—to call the Pennington County Sheriff's Department. The dispatcher promised to send a car within the next half hour.

Feeling a bit braver knowing that backup was on the way, she clipped the phone to the waistband of her khaki capris—she'd worn her standard summer uniform that included a bright purple T-shirt over tan bottoms—and walked to the room's lone window. She nudged aside the plastic miniblinds. From this angle, she couldn't see all of the buildings, but she had a clear view of Dizzy.

Her father originally had named the exhibit "The Paradox," which he'd explained was an apparent contradiction relating to physical evidence. "I think you should call it Dizzy," she'd cried, staggering drunkenly as she crossed what appeared to be an even floor. "'Cause that's how it makes me feel."

She tensed, squinting to see into the shadows. Was that a person edging suspiciously toward the side window of the building?

Yes. And the man's height, weight and body type were an almost certain match for the person who had walked into Char's shop the day before with Cooper Lindstrom. Shane somebody. Her mother's Bernese mountain dog.

Still dressed in black, he moved with athletic grace. She didn't know if Coop was around, too, or why they were there, but she didn't think either of them was dangerous. She had a keen intuition about bad men—the only good thing to come out of the attack that changed her life during her sophomore year of college.

"Never go looking for trouble," her personal-defense instructor had stressed, "but if trouble taps you on the shoulder, take it down."

SHANE HEARD a scratching sound from inside the building. Looking up, he spotted an open double-hung window. On the ground below, he could see a few shards of glass.

Okay, he thought. Breaking and entering. Definitely time to call the cops.

He pulled out his phone and called 9-1-1.

Nothing happened.

He looked at the signal indicator. No service. He swore to himself. Coop had complained about the spotty reception in the Hills, but Shane had assumed his pal was exaggerating to explain dodging Shane's calls.

He returned the phone to his pocket and debated what to do. If he drove back to town, the guy inside would be long gone by the time the authorities showed up. But confronting a burglar without backup was insane. The guy could be on crack or something.

"Damn," he muttered.

There was a third option, of course. Wait until the guy came out and take down his description. He frowned. Maybe he'd been working in Hollywood too long, but the idea sounded both lame and cowardly. Besides, with the racket the guy was making inside, he might destroy the place while Shane waited.

Taking a deep breath, he put one foot on the water meter or whatever the gray contraption was beneath the window and stepped up. He tried to balance without touching the ledge since silvery shards sparkled in the black metal frame. *The perp was smart enough to know to wear gloves,* he thought.

"Okay. Stop right now and I won't press charges," a voice said from behind him.

Shane turned his head just as a flash of movement from

inside the building caught his eye. He looked back and forth so quickly, he lost his balance. He grabbed for the sill and felt several sharp pricks that made him yelp. Reacting instinctively, he let go about the same time the soles of his shoes slipped on the dewy surface of the pipe he'd been standing on. He backpedaled gracelessly, his hip grazing the metal object as he fell. He hit the ground hard.

His curse was long, low and heartfelt.

"If you'd read the protocol sign before you broke in, you'd know that swearing isn't allowed in the Mystery Spot," an unsympathetic voice said.

He looked up. Jenna.

"I didn't break in," he said, making small movements to see if anything was broken. "The guy inside did. I just followed to see what he was up to."

One reddish eyebrow arched in obvious skepticism.

"Why would I break in to this place?"

"I was trying to figure that out myself…when I called the police. They're on the way."

He rolled to his side and sat up. A good sign, he figured. Spreading his fingers wide, he looked at his palm where at least five red specks were screaming in pain. "Glass," he muttered, holding his hand up for her to see.

"You should have worn gloves."

"I didn't—"

His protest was cut short by the sound of a loud bang. *Gunshot.*

He reacted without thinking. He dove forward, catching her at the knees, which knocked her backward. Doing a quick combat crawl, he flattened her beneath him.

She stayed still for less than half a second then exploded in a whirling dervish of legs, arms, claws and thrusts. Her knee made contact with his groin and he rolled off, curling in a ball, groaning—the pain in his hand forgotten.

"What the hell did you do that for?" she asked, scrambling backward, crablike.

Through his tears, he saw her. Face as white as flour. Eyes wild with panic, and she was breathing as if she'd just run a marathon.

He'd interviewed rape survivors while making his first documentary. He knew the signs of post-traumatic stress. And he wished like hell he'd never met Cooper Lindstrom.

The sound of tires crunching gravel brought her to her feet. She raced away, red hair streaming behind. Inching sideways, he picked up a turquoise clip that had fallen out of her hair. In trying to save her from a bullet, he'd landed on his right palm and he could tell without looking the hunk of glass was now deeply imbedded in his flesh.

In hindsight, he figured the sound had been a door slamming. The person who broke the window and took down the boards in the fence had been smart enough to open the door from the inside and run away once he heard voices.

Shane felt ridiculous. Things like this didn't happen to him. He took risks when it came to work, but not when it came to his personal life. And the last time he'd even talked to a cop was back in college. When his brother raped Jenna Murphy.

And then he'd unwittingly lied to provide his twin with an alibi.

CHAPTER THREE

THE DEPUTY SHERIFF SEEMED curious, professional and only a wee bit impressed when Shane mentioned his reason for being in Sentinel Pass. His main concern was the property damage and trespassing.

Jenna quickly assured him that she had no complaint against Shane, but the man walked the entire perimeter of the Mystery Spot once Shane showed him the photo he'd taken of a shadowy figure doing something to the fence. Other than the boards still lying where Shane had found them and the broken window, there didn't appear to be any trace of the intruder.

"You back up to Forest Service land?" the cop asked, poking his head out the opening to look left and right.

"Yes. Dad wanted something that wouldn't be developed. He felt it gave more veracity to our setting. You know, a true fluke of nature, breaking all the rules of QED. Quantum Electrodynamics," she added for both men's benefit.

The officer helped Shane lean the boards back in place. "I've got a hammer in the office," Jenna said. "I'll take care of this before I leave."

They started back in that general direction. The officer smiled. "My wife and I brought our kids here a few years ago. They had a blast in the maze. I was afraid they'd never come out. You're sure nothing is missing or vandalized?"

"Everything appears to be fine. Except for the window. Oh, and the broken lock on the storage cabinet inside Dizzy. Guess that supply of window cleaner and toilet paper wasn't worth stealing."

"Got someone you can call to take care of the glass?"

"I'll make sure it gets fixed," Shane said, not exactly certain what he was promising. True, his uncle had been a self-employed handyman, and Shane and Adam had had the option of working with the kind, older man every summer. Adam had hated it and mostly goofed off whenever Uncle John wasn't watching, but Shane had enjoyed working with his hands and had learned quite a few tricks of the trade that had kept him fed until he sold his first screenplay.

Jenna gaped at him as if he'd just declared he would strip naked and swing from the trees. "My uncle was a self-proclaimed jack-of-all-trades, master of none. He taught me a thing or two," he explained. "But if you don't trust me to do it, I'm sure I can hire it done."

The deputy left a few minutes later. He said he'd file a report and to call if the culprit returned. Both he and Jenna seemed to think the perpetrator was a bored kid, probably acting on a dare. Shane disagreed. The image in the photo he'd snapped showed a person close to Shane's size, not a preteen with too much time on his hands. But even the most desperate junkie would know the pickings in a place like this would be pretty slim, so what was the guy looking for? Shane didn't have an answer.

Once the sound of the patrol car's tires crossing the

gravel had faded, Jenna motioned for Shane to follow her
to the largest of the buildings. Like the one they'd been
standing beside, it was painted chocolate-brown with shiny
green shutters that apparently could be latched during the
off-season.

"We used to have kids break in during the winter when
we were closed," Jenna said, leading the way. "That's why
Dad had the shutters made."

"But the shutters are open."

"It's summer. Our high season. Normally," she added
with a sigh.

"Are you usually working here?"

She'd tucked her hair behind her ears. Shane still had
her clip in his pocket. He knew he should give it back,
but…he didn't.

"Yep. Twelve/seven from the end of May to Labor Day.
We're open nine in the morning to nine at night."

"That's grueling. You do this alone?"

"No. I hire high school and college kids. About twenty
of them since they all want to work in the beginning but
not so much toward the end of summer. I understand. I felt
the same when I was their age."

Their age. College age. He really needed to tell her who
he was.

"I suppose you're wondering why I'm here."

She skirted the main entrance, which was recessed and
painted black with images from space—stars, planets,
galaxies and nebulas. The artwork was cheesy at best, but
what caught his attention were the large, Plexiglas display
cases that flanked the opening. Even from a distance he
could make out some familiar faces: Einstein, Stephen
Hawking and Isaac Newton. There were others he couldn't

place, but their names seemed vaguely familiar—like answers to *Jeopardy* questions under the category of Famous Scientists.

She unlocked the door of a small lean-to—about the size of a one-car garage tucked behind a large flowering bush. "I keep a first-aid kit in here," she said motioning him forward. "I've had people pass out in Dizzy—the building you were peeking into. One lady panicked in the maze and ran smack into the wall. She had a huge goose egg above her eye but refused to let me call the paramedics. She insisted she had to see Crazy Horse."

She glanced over her shoulder and smiled. Her smile made him feel a little shaky. Maybe he had a concussion.

"Sit in my chair," she said, pointing to a chair that looked like something his uncle would have owned. The worn leather upholstery had been repaired with Duct tape.

"This is your office?"

"Heart and soul of the operation, although my dad would have begged to say otherwise. Originally, he wanted the Mystery Spot to be free so schoolkids could get excited about physics." She gave him a wry smile that seemed to say, "Like that would ever happen."

He sat, glad to be off his feet. "I saw the sign. There's an admission fee." Modest, to be sure. He didn't know if that was all the market could bear or if the tour wasn't worth any more.

"Yeah, well, Mom finally convinced him it was okay to make enough money to pay the help and property taxes. He always put every dime of profit back into the place. He'd probably still be building new exhibits if he hadn't died."

"I lost my father, too. We weren't close," he added hoping to forgo any expression of sympathy.

"Is your mother still alive?"

He shook his head. "She's been gone almost six years."

She took a plastic box with a large red cross on the cover from a built-in cabinet and returned to where he was sitting. The room was so small she couldn't move without him smelling her perfume. He didn't recognize the scent but he liked it. When he'd known her in college she'd worn Charlie. This was better—fresh and vibrant with just a hint of exotic.

"Were the two of you close?" Her tone let him know she'd picked up on his brusque comment about his father.

Two peas in a pod, Mom had called them when Shane was a little boy. A highly dysfunctional pod, he'd later come to understand.

To avoid answering the question, he said, "I read some of your poetry this morning. Coop lent me his copy of your book."

She let out a low groan. "You poor man. First my collegiate musings, then a fist full of glass. I wonder which was more painful." She turned his hand palm up and rested it on the corner of the desk.

"I don't know much about poetry, but I thought they showed a very strong voice."

"Strong?" She was close enough for him to see the flecks of gold he'd always found so fascinating in her predominantly green eyes. "That's an interesting choice of words, given the time in my life when I wrote them. But other people have said that, too."

She glanced up for a millisecond then pushed her glasses back to the bridge of her nose and leaned closer to his hand. "The book caused a huge rift in my family. I almost disowned my mother because she sent those poems to a publisher without my permission. And my dad was outraged because it cost a small fortune to produce."

"Ouch."

She looked at him. "I haven't done anything, yet."

He was pretty sure she knew what he'd meant but he smiled anyway. "There's a law against publishing other people's work. It's called copyright."

The shoulders of her purple T-shirt lifted and fell. "I guess she figured if they were in a box under a bed in her house, then they were free game. She claims it was her way of liberating me from my nightmares."

She suffered from nightmares? "Did it work?"

She didn't answer right away. When she did, her voice sounded bemused. "Well…pretty much."

How strange, he thought. If his mother had ever submitted his youthful short stories somewhere without his permission, he'd have killed her. No. That wasn't true. She'd done something far, far worse, and he'd still held her hand and told her he loved her as she took her last breath.

"Does this hurt?" she asked, lightly swabbing the gash in his palm with a cotton ball dipped in alcohol.

"Not bad."

She sucked in her top lip, eyes narrowed as she moved his hand closer to the lamp on her desk. "Well, this will. There's a piece of glass under the skin. Brace yourself."

She sterilized the tweezers, doused the skin a second time then went to work. He flinched. He couldn't help himself. The pain was sharp, but she didn't mess around. She pulled out the tiny shard and dropped it in a metal waste basket. "There. I think you'll heal fine."

"Thanks."

"You're welcome." She stood. "Let that air-dry a minute

then I'll put some antibacterial ointment on it and a bandage. I have a certain silly yellow cartoon character in three sizes of strips if you ask nicely," she said, returning to the cabinet.

He snickered softly. "Gee, thanks."

She moved some items on a shelf and poked around for another minute or two before tamping her hands on her hips. "I give up. Where did the ointment go?"

He enjoyed watching her decision-making process. Her clear, milky-white skin reminded him of a porcelain doll his mother had cherished. The day of the funeral, when he went to her room to retrieve the small memento she'd left him, he'd found it on the floor of her bathroom, smashed to pieces.

"Don't take this wrong. I'm not being judgmental, honestly, but when I read your poems, I got a sense that you weren't too thrilled with men. Is that just me or should I be worried about that pair of scissors in your hand?"

She looked at the object she'd picked up but obviously hadn't realized she was holding. She dropped the shears on the shelf and turned to face him. Her grin told him she didn't plan to murder him. "You're very perceptive. Men were my personal anti-Christ when I wrote those poems. I'd just dropped out of college and was living at home again. My dad, who was a tenured professor with a Ph.D., was on my case about returning to school, so I took a creative writing class. To piss him off."

"He didn't like writing?"

"He was a man of science. He considered the arts frivolous."

"How open-minded of him," he said wryly. "So, did this class achieve its objective?"

She scratched her cheek as if giving the question serious thought. "Well, my teacher was a fervent feminist who had been raped when she was a young mother. The class could have been called Poetry That Proves All Men Are Jerks."

Shane coughed. "Were there any men in the class?"

"A few. And, interestingly, they never tried to defend their sex. I guess men can be cruel to other men, too."

Wasn't that the truth? He could have named a dozen times that he'd seen Adam publicly humiliate perfect strangers, usually men. Although he'd put down his share of women, too. Yet women flocked to him. Even the smart ones. Like Jenna.

"What did you do when you found out your mother submitted your work to a publisher?"

She took a wide adhesive strip out of a box then turned to look at him. "We're not talking a *real* publisher. This vanity press had no qualms about taking my mother's money even though she wasn't the author. My dad threatened to sue, but the company declared bankruptcy and disappeared before he could follow through." After applying the bandage, she cocked her head and sighed. "You don't have a clever craft project that requires several dozen boxes of worthless books, do you? I thought they might make an interesting lamp base, but I've never been able to find the right kind of glue."

Her tone was blasé but Shane heard an undercurrent of something most people would have missed. He'd worked with actors too long. He could tell when someone was faking it.

"Jenna, I need to tell you something before this gets really awkward. You don't remember me, but we met years ago. In college. We had an art appreciation class together. I was a senior. You were a freshman."

"Sophomore," she corrected. "That was one of the classes I didn't finish. Eventually the professor worked with me through the mail and I managed to get the incomplete changed to a B."

She put a little more space between them, discreetly inching closer to the door. Her gaze bore into him. "When you first walked into the store yesterday, I thought you looked familiar, but I just assumed I'd seen you on TV. Like Coop."

He shook his head. "Nope. I'm a behind-the-scenes kind of guy. Would it help if I told you I had a ponytail in college? And a full beard." He made Os with his thumbs and fingers and held them up to his eyes. "And thick glasses."

Her jaw dropped and she inhaled sharply. "You're *that* Shane? Long-haired, pot-smoking, artsy-fartsy Shane Osterman...Osterberg—"

"Ostergren," he supplied, smiling at her description of him. He'd been all those things. A rebel without a clue. "I changed my name when I moved to L.A."

"Why?"

The million-answer question. "I usually tell people I was afraid I might wind up producing porn," he said lamely. "But mostly I didn't want my name associated with my family...and vice versa. My dad was in politics at the time."

She processed the information for a minute before asking, "Why Reynard?"

"My mother's maiden name, plus I thought it sounded French and edgy."

Her pretty, Angelina Jolie lips pursed. "It means fox, you know. Although it's spelled differently, if I remember correctly from Mrs. Haver's French class."

"You're right. No *y*. I looked it up a couple of years ago because Coop insisted the word meant duck."

She grinned. "*Canard. Renard.* Easy mistake to make. And the former can be a verb as well as a farm animal." Her green eyes flashed with humor. "Which could explain your reaction when you thought we were being shot at."

He hooted softly, impressed by both her quick wit and her sexy accent. "Habit."

"You've been shot at before?"

"Drive-by's are common in L.A. Fortunately, not in my current neighborhood, but when I first moved there, Coop and I rented a place that was on the fringe of gang territory. We heard gunshots nightly."

"You've been friends a long time."

He noticed she'd adroitly steered the topic away from their college years. "Like you and Libby."

"Actually, Libby and I have known each other since junior high. We spent every summer together. Her grandmother was busy at the post office and my mom worked the gate while my dad gave tours. Later on, Lib and I would give tours. Boys whose parents dragged them to the Mystery Spot would hit on us. It was fun. We even met kids from other countries."

"Is that why you studied French?"

She seemed surprised by the question. "I suppose," she mumbled, reaching for the faded pink backpack he'd seen sitting just inside the door. "I, um, have a health inspector coming in a few minutes. I should probably make sure all the paperwork is in order."

A polite way of saying, Scram.

"What do you plan to do about setting up motion detectors or installing an alarm system?"

She pulled a manila file out of the bag. "It's on the list," she said. "Right after I pay for the new water system we just put in, get the parking lot paved and reroof all the buildings."

"Oh."

Brilliant reply, genius, he heard his brother snicker.

He'd come here hoping to find some peace of mind where Jenna was concerned. It crossed his mind to offer to pay for any or all of those things, but what would he say when she asked why he felt he needed to give her money?

A guilty conscience, he'd be forced to admit.

For what? For not sticking around the party longer? For not deflecting his brother's attention? For unintentionally providing his brother with an alibi?

He couldn't break his promise to his mother. Besides, Adam was a powerful man with powerful friends. Maybe Jenna was better off not knowing the truth. Shane had learned at a very young age that the adage, Let Sleeping Dogs Lie definitely applied to his brother. Shane had the scars to prove it.

"Why don't I give you a lift into town after your meeting? You can't carry a new piece of glass on your bike."

"I have a car. Mom needed it this morning, but she should be back by the time I get home. Thanks for offering, though. And I'm sorry about kneeing you. My self-defense training sort of took over."

"It worked," he said, feeling a twinge in his groin as he got to his feet. "You took a class because of what happened to you in college, right?"

She frowned. "You heard about that, huh?"

He didn't tell her that everyone on campus had talked

about little else for a solid week. "I tried to visit you at the hospital. My car wouldn't start so I was hoofing it. I remember I was by McCrory Gardens when I saw you in the backseat of your parents' car. I've never forgotten the look on your face."

Even now, the image that came to mind made an intense fire start to burn in his gut. Rage, hopelessness and despair—triggered by the disillusionment and emptiness he'd seen in her eyes.

Her narrow, perfectly groomed eyebrows arched in disbelief. "You're kidding, right? I pretty much blanked out everything about that time once I got my feelings down on paper. Therapy by poetry, my teacher called it."

He dug in his pocket for his sunglasses. Had they fallen out when he hit the ground or were they still in the car? He felt naked without them. "I should go."

"I seem to remember Coop and my mother talking about you. The movies you'd made. Didn't one of them deal with violence against women?"

"Yeah, but it was an indie. Not widely released. You probably didn't see it."

"I wouldn't have gone to it back then, anyway. It took me years to get enough perspective on the subject. Even my closest friends—except for Libby—don't know about the rape. I didn't want pain and fear to define my life."

"Sounds smart. I'm glad you've put what happened behind you."

She shrugged. "All things being relative. I never got my degree. I started back a couple of times. My dad kept harping at me. But even he gave up when I flunked four out of five classes, including bowling."

"If it makes you feel any better, I never went back, either."

"And according to Coop, you're a successful producer, director and screenwriter. Maybe I should have given Hollywood a try." She tried to sound flippant but couldn't quite pull it off. "Instead, I went to Montana to live with my aunt. I worked at a grain elevator. It was actually kind of interesting, but then Dad…"

"Ah, yes, the demands of family."

The bitterness in his tone raised a whole slew of questions, but before she could ask even one, the sound of tires on gravel interrupted. She opened the door and looked out. "White truck. Must be the inspector." She glanced at her watch. "Amazingly prompt. I figured I'd be sitting here all day."

She expected him to use this avenue to escape but once again he did the unexpected. He picked up the folder she'd dropped on the desk and tucked it under his arm. "Tell me again, what exactly is he inspecting?"

An hour later she wondered if her luck was changing. The inspection passed without a single correction. Of course, that might have had something to do with Shane's presence. Once it clicked who Shane was, the man with the clipboard barely glanced at her shiny new pipes. Instead of making certain her soldered joints were properly soldered, he regaled Shane with his acting experience as a member of the Black Hills Repertory.

Shane handled the man with such finesse Jenna was convinced the guy believed he had a shot at a career in Hollywood.

"Did you just offer him a tryout in L.A.?" she asked, glancing at the green tag the man had given her before he left.

"No."

"He thinks you did."

"That was the idea."

They were standing near the lumpy pile of reddish clay that had been excavated a few weeks earlier. Jenna was keeping her fingers crossed that Walt was back from Denver and available to backfill the hole, now that they had permission to turn on their water.

"What will you do if he quits his job and shows up knocking on your door?" she asked.

He looked at her, humor dancing in his eyes even if he wasn't smiling. "He won't. Believe me. If he were as dedicated to his craft as he wanted us to believe, he'd already be there. This was just small talk."

She wasn't sure she was comfortable with his ability to read minds.

"So, are you done here? If you get me a hammer, I'll renail those boards, then take you into town for a piece of glass. I really don't feel comfortable leaving you here alone."

The Mystery Spot was the one place on the planet that she'd always felt safe. After the rape, which had taken place at the end of October, she'd come home to recuperate. To escape her mother's hovering and her father's nagging, she'd come to the Mystery Spot with a heavy quilt and an empty notebook.

The following January, she'd transferred to Black Hills State—in theory. She couldn't list how many times she'd skipped classes to hide out here. But when midterm grades showed up, she'd had to deal with the flack from her father who simply didn't understand why she couldn't "get back on her horse," as he put it. Education had been the cornerstone of his belief system. To have a daughter flunk even one class was unthinkable.

She'd left Sentinel Pass the following fall rather than face his disappointment when she didn't go back to school.

"That's not necessary. I've been known to swing a hammer, and I'm sure someone at the hardware store could replace the glass for me. Besides, the inspector's shameless self-promotion was mild compared to what my mother might say or do if she were home when we got there. She used to be an actress."

"It comes with the job," he said carelessly, holding out his hand. "Where's your hammer?"

She didn't know why he was so concerned about what happened to her, but she'd felt unsettled since Libby's call that morning—and, in truth, she was a little freaked out by the break-in. She'd learned a long time ago to listen to her instincts, and whose instincts seemed pretty comfortable with Shane from college, so she made a gut call. "Stay here. I'll get it."

She was back in under a minute, and they walked around the side of Dizzy to find the breach. Neither spoke at first, then Shane said, "I don't usually tell people what I do for a living. If someone asks, I tell them I'm a screenwriter. Which is what I still do. But I never admit to being a director."

"Why?"

"I was once hit up for a part by the woman cleaning my teeth. Talk about being in a compromising position."

She found it refreshing that he didn't seem to take himself too seriously. "Well, Mom's got too much pride to do something like that. But she does love to reminisce about the past. And if she likens you to a dog..." She shrugged. "Consider it a compliment. You're her favorite breed."

"I have no idea what that means, but as Coop said last night, we are looking for some local talent to use in bit parts. If your mother can act, I might be able to find a place for her in the cast."

Jenna didn't say anything. She couldn't imagine her mother on television, but that might be her personal bias talking. She couldn't wait to share this news with the other members of the Wine, Women and Words book club. At least, she hoped they were still on for tonight. Libby hadn't mentioned canceling when they'd spoken that morning, but things might have changed with Cooper back in town.

Jenna would call the other members as soon as she got home. She wondered what they'd make of the fact that she and Shane had attended the same college. And even more remarkable, he'd been there when her life went to hell.

"Are we done here?" he asked.

"Yes. I think so. Thank you. How's your hand?"

He rubbed a finger across the shiny strip. "Perfect." He handed her the hammer. "I'm going to my car to see if I left my sunglasses on the seat. Do you want to meet me there after you lock up?"

"Sure. I'll be right there."

As she walked away, she felt that old, familiar pang— a mix of regret, deep sadness and wistfulness. How strange to run into Shane here after all these years. He'd been one of the most intriguing people she'd met in college. Dark, brooding, "Heathcliffesque" she remembered calling him to one of her friends.

If not for what happened that night, she might have eventually gotten up the nerve to talk to him. Maybe. He'd interested her, but she'd been fully aware of the fact he was so not the kind of guy her dad would have wanted her to date. And she'd so valued her father's opinion that when she saw Shane at the off-campus frat party, she'd immediately turned her attention to a handsome, clean-cut stranger.

She never in a million years would have guessed he was Shane's twin brother. She didn't even believe Adam at first, but he knew so much about Shane, told the funniest stories. She'd let down her guard and had fun. Too much fun. Too many beers. And the last one was spiked with a new drug that was supposed to lower inhibitions. A date-rape drug, they called it. She hadn't been on a date, but she had been raped.

Old news. Ancient history. And she planned to keep it that way.

CHAPTER FOUR

THE CAR WAS SPACIOUS and new smelling. National Public Radio was playing on the radio, but Shane turned it off before stepping on the gas. She liked that. He had nice manners.

"So, you've passed this stage of the fix-it game," he said, driving slowly across the parking lot. "When will you open for business again?"

"Hopefully this weekend. We posted one of our best weekends ever during the Memorial Day holiday. Then, suddenly, the water line broke. I'm just praying my young employees haven't all found new jobs."

He stopped at the gate and got out to replace the cone. She watched him in the side mirror. He took extra care to make certain her hand-printed sign was visible.

She still couldn't quite get over the fact that he was the same Shane from college. He certainly looked different, although he was still gorgeous and intriguing.

Warning bells went off in her head. Since when did intriguing men appeal to her? Never. She liked safe men. Like her old friend, Mac. There was nothing safe about this particular Bernese mountain dog. He had more of a Doberman look to her.

She swallowed the giggle that bubbled up from her

throat. Oh, God, she was becoming her mother. Next, she'd start carrying baby aspirin in her purse.

Once he was back in the car, he resumed his questions about her business. "So, you were open for one weekend, and then your plumbing broke?"

She coughed into her fist to hide her grin. Her mother referred to female ailments as "delicate plumbing problems." "Walt—my plumber—said the line may have had a stress fracture from the last thaw. I looked into renting portable toilets in the interim, but the Health Department insisted we needed running water before we could reopen."

"If the plumber isn't available, do you have someone else you could call to backfill the trench?"

She thought a moment. "Mac, Libby's brother, would probably do it, but I'm hoping Walt is back in town. He needs the money." She explained about his daughter's accident. "This has been tough on the family. I'm not sure they had insurance."

He shook his head. "I understand, but if he's not around, Coop and I could help out."

She shifted in the seat to face him. "Why would you volunteer to do that? Somehow I don't picture you or Cooper as the hands-on shovel types."

His ruddy complexion darkened a shade. "Like I told you, I learned a few things from my uncle. I'm no stranger to hard work."

That still didn't answer her question as to why he was so interested in helping her. Maybe he felt sorry for her. Because of her past. The rape was probably the last thing he ever heard about her, and her stupid book of poetry probably hadn't helped. He must regard her as some kind of charity case.

She changed the subject. "Am I right in remembering that you're from Minnesota? You said your parents are both gone, but you have a brother, right? I met him. He said you—"

He cut her off. "Is this the right way? Coop claimed it was impossible to get lost around here, but then he told me about hiking for hours in the wrong direction, so I'm not putting much stock in what he says."

She remembered the day he was talking about. She'd been the idiot who had volunteered to pick up Coop and Libby at the trail's end. They'd arrived over two hours late and dog dead tired.

But apparently not too exhausted to fool around, she thought fighting back a grin. "Different area. And, yes, this is the right road. Do you like to hike?"

"Me? Hike? Never tried it. Mostly I work."

"You look pretty fit for someone who doesn't exercise." She clapped her hand over her mouth. "Oh, nuts, that's just the kind of too-personal observation my mother tends to make—usually at my expense."

His casual shrug let her off the hook. "I'll take it as a compliment. I have a gym at my house, and a pool. My mother died of colon cancer, and my dad had complications from a stroke. I try to take care of myself."

She couldn't imagine losing her mother, too. She quickly turned to face forward again. "There's the turn off for the Little Poke. I wonder if Mac is working today," she said, idly.

He took his foot off the gas. "Mac is Libby's brother, right?"

She nodded. "Short for Marshall Amos Coolidge McGannon. A combination of his father's name and mother's maiden name. His late wife's name was Misty and she took the whole *M* thing to another level by naming their daughter Megan. Poor Mac was mortified, but he never denied that woman anything."

That woman. Shane read a wealth of content into her tone. Jenna hadn't cared for her best friend's late sister-in-law. *Curious…*

"If you turn at the next corner," she said, pointing to the right, "we can take the back way to my house. I'm anxious to get the glass ordered. Smart of you to suggest taking the exact measurements."

He shrugged. "No problem. Will my cell phone work at your house?"

"Probably," she said. "A lot of people in town have cell phones. I've resisted getting one because we don't have reception at the Spot, but I've actually had some people tell me they can call out from the parking lot…if the azimuth of the sun is just right," she added, grinning. "I invested in a Mystery Spot Web site last year. That pretty much gobbled up my new technology budget."

"Oh." He made the turn down a street that lacked curb and gutter. And streetlights. "I should have checked you out on the Internet."

"It turned out pretty good I think. Lots of pictures, a couple interactive games and a bunch of scientific links for teachers to download. My dad would have liked it." She sat forward, squinting. "Mom's home. If you want to stop here, I'll hop out."

He ignored the suggestion. He'd noticed that she'd returned the glasses she'd used to read the inspector's paperwork to a case in her backpack after the man left. He'd assumed that meant she was farsighted, but maybe vanity kept her from wearing glasses all the time. He knew all about that, having worn glasses since the time he was five. Adam had perfect vision.

"Listen, I love my mom to pieces—really, I do—but she's not everybody's cup of tea. If the trip down memory lane becomes torturous, feel free to make the first lame excuse that comes to mind and bail. Also, it's probably wise to stay away from questions about health or ill—"

She wasn't able to complete the warning because a voice called from the porch with surprising force and clarity given the size of the woman shouting. "You're back early. Who's that with you? Oh, my Lord, is that the Bernese mountain dog?"

Shane looked at Jenna, who blushed all the way to the roots of her red hair. "Mother," she mumbled, using the three-syllable version of the word.

She wouldn't make eye contact with him but got out once he'd put the car in Park. "Mom, meet Shane Reynard. Shane, my mother, Bess Murphy."

The woman, who was wearing a linen pantsuit the color of weak tea with a ruby blouse and Jackson Pollockesque silk scarf at her neck, looked as if she'd just had tea with the governor. She gracefully floated down the steps, one hand out as if she expected him to kiss it.

He quickly hopped out of the car to meet her.

"Mary Margaret Murphy," she corrected, shaking his hand as firmly as many men of his acquaintance. "That's my stage name. I've never forgiven my late husband for giving me that bovine nickname. Now that's all anybody calls me."

"It could be worse," Jenna said. "In private, Dad used to call her Bessie."

Bess glared at her. "Watch it, young lady. I'll…" She stopped. Frowning, she sighed. "Oh, Lord, I've run out of retributions. Now, she's the one giving me an allowance."

"It's called a budget, Mom."

"Well, we won't have to worry about that once I start acting again, will we?"

Shane looked at Jenna, whose expressive face showed nothing but concern. She didn't say anything, however, and her mother started toward the house. "May I offer you a cup of coffee, Shane? You don't mind if I call you by your first name, do you? I feel so old when I find myself using *mister* to address men my daughter's age."

"Shane is fine. And I'd love a cup of coffee. I'm about a pint low. I'll be right there. First I need to give Jenna the measurements for the new piece of glass."

Bess stopped and looked at Jenna. "Glass? What glass?"

"There's a broken window in Dizzy. Some kid—"

Before she could finish, her mother cut her off. "Another expense. Just what we don't need. Jenna, I'm beginning to think it's time we sell that albatross and move on with our lives."

Shane had no trouble reading the shock in her daughter's expression. Jenna obviously hadn't been expecting that bombshell.

Her mother disappeared into the house without waiting for a reply. Shane had to give the woman credit. Her exit was perfect dramatic timing. The audience would have gasped, as Jenna did, then been left with bated anticipation for the next scene.

He grabbed the scrap of paper with the measurements, then locked the car and walked to where Jenna was standing.

She took the paper without glancing at it. "Thank you."

"I take it that suggestion came out of the blue?"

She shrugged. "It's the first time she's said the words, but there have been clues. Like the fact that she doesn't want to work there anymore. Last year she took more sick days than any of the teens on my payroll. I think it's safe to assume all this talk about Hollywood has rekindled her hopes of an acting career."

"You don't think that's a good idea."

She looked at him and frowned. "It's like what you said about the inspector today. If acting was really her calling, shouldn't she have done something to make it happen by now? She hasn't auditioned for a single role since my dad died. What does that tell you?"

"Maybe she's still mourning."

She hesitated as if weighing her words carefully. "My father was a wonderful man, and I think Mom and Dad were very much in love the whole time they were married. But any time Mom would show an interest in trying out for a play or the summer dinner theater, something would come up—being shorthanded at the Spot, for instance—that kept her from doing it."

Shane sensed something in her voice that didn't have to do with her mother. "Did he do the same thing about your writing?"

"My writing." Her laugh was brittle and edgy. "Dad believed everyone should have a hobby—his was the Mystery Spot—as long as it didn't interfere with their *real* life's work. I thought he was going to have a heart attack when I told him I was attending a liberal arts college instead of going to the School of Mines."

"My father wanted me to go into law," he said.

Neither said anything for a moment. Long enough for Shane to make an impulsive decision he knew he'd regret later. But she looked so lost and blue, as if the marvelous possibilities of the past were shadows of butterflies shifting on the breeze out of reach. "Listen, I know that summer is your busy season, but I was hoping to hire someone local to help me with the scripts Cooper and I are supposed to be writing. Are you interested?"

Coop had been the first to suggest hiring her, but Shane had dismissed the idea as mildly insane and ridiculously masochistic given what his brother did to her and knowing how he'd once felt about her. "A few hours a day. I pay really well. And this would be a chance to prove that your dad was wrong."

She looked at him a second, then took a deep breath, let it out and turned toward the house. "I need to get this glass ordered. Are you coming in?"

So much for his offer. Either the idea was too crazy to warrant a response or she didn't think he was serious. And maybe he was nuts to consider it. The less he had to do with her, the less chance of her putting together what happened that night before he could make amends.

But he liked being around her, damn it. He still missed the girl she'd been, and had been tempted by the glimpses of that girl he'd caught this morning. Something he could easily become addicted to.

He followed after her.

"Mom, did Libby call again?" she asked, holding the door for Shane.

"Yes. I just listened to the message. She wants to know if they could have book club here, instead of at her house."

"Hmm…is that okay with you?"

Bess, who held a thick album crushed to her chest like a holy tablet, motioned with her chin for Shane to join her. "Yes, of course. I'll stay upstairs with Alec and Vanna."

"Trebec and White," Jenna supplied as he walked past her. "Game shows." She'd stopped in the foyer beside a marble-topped table where an old-fashioned phone shared space with an answering machine. On odd mix of old and new, he thought.

"Got it."

Her mother handed him the album, then pressed him to sit on the overstuffed sofa. "I'll be right back," she promised, regally sashaying into the adjoining kitchen.

He looked around. White walls with wallpaper wainscot that looked a bit past its prime. Brass lamps and collage frames conspired to give the place a 1980s sitcom studio set feel.

She returned with two flowery mugs on a tray with a matching ceramic cream and sugar bowl made to look like a cow and calf. "You look familiar, Shane," she said, sitting beside him. "Have we met?"

Not the question Shane had expected. A history of her acting accomplishments, maybe. Or inquiries about Coop and the TV project. Not an intense scrutiny that made him reach for his sunglasses. Damn, he'd left them in the car again. "I don't think so."

"Then I must have seen you in a trade magazine or on a talk show. I never forget a face. Or an actor in a role. I have an amazing memory for such things, if I do say so myself."

He accepted the mug she offered but declined either additive. "I've never acted. I prefer to stay behind the scenes. Writing, producing, directing."

She stirred her spoon with a dainty flare. "Cooper

mentioned you the last time he was here. Funny that my mind somehow imagined you just as you are. All in black. But with soulful brown eyes. I wasn't expecting the slightly haunted look in your eyes, though."

He gulped his coffee—and burned the top of mouth. "Speaking of Coop, I should probably check in with him." He reached into his pocket for his phone, but it wasn't there.

She made a placating gesture. "Oh, don't get skittish just because I speak what's on my mind. Life's too short to pretend, don't you think? Unless you're on stage. That's what I loved best about acting. Then I could be anybody. I don't suppose you're looking for someone like me to be in your show, are you? I play a mean, quirky older woman. Do you know Olympia Dukakis?"

He blew on his coffee and tried another sip. "Not personally."

"She's my inspiration. I tell Jenna if you ever need a role model for someone who never gives up on a dream, that's the lady to look at. I haven't been on the boards in years— even before Jenna's father died I'd more or less retired— but…well, sometimes I think about Olympia and feel guilty that I didn't try harder."

Coop had mentioned Jenna's mother several times when he'd been here earlier. He'd called her a character. Shane was beginning to see his point. He liked her—even if the all-knowing look in her eyes left him slightly unnerved.

"You know, I really can't say at the moment because, unfortunately, I don't have a script," he said. "Coop and I are supposed to be working on one this week, but I don't know how much help he's going to be."

His stomach made an unhappy sound, and it wasn't

because he was hungry. If they didn't get something on paper this week, the network execs would probably yank control of the project right out of Shane's hands. Not something Shane was about to let happen. People didn't call him a control freak for nothing.

"Cooper gave me a copy of your daughter's book of poetry. I don't suppose she writes prose, does she?"

Bess leaned closer and said softly, "On the sly. I'm not supposed to know. She doesn't tell anyone. Even Libby."

"Then how do you know?"

"I'm her mother. Two women in the same house have very few secrets from each other." He waited knowing there was more. "Plus, I might have accidentally glanced at her notebook one day."

She wrote in longhand? He didn't know anyone who didn't use a computer, but he supposed that made sense to someone who grew up believing creativity was something suspect. He knew she wasn't a Luddite. She'd mentioned making a Web site for the Mystery Spot.

"How's the grilling going?" Jenna asked, popping her head in from the other room. Shane had heard the soft murmur of her voice on the phone and assumed she'd been able to place the order. "I see you haven't had to resort to dental tools to get him to talk, Mom."

"A bit esoteric, Jenna Mae. Your movie reference probably went right over his head."

"You mean *Marathon Man?*" Shane asked. "Dustin Hoffman takes on a Nazi war criminal. I still get shivers picturing the moment…who was the actor who drilled into his tooth?"

Bess's eyes opened wide. "Laurence Olivier, 1976. Oh, he's good, Jenna. Let's keep him. I bet we'd win every tournament."

He looked at Jenna.

"Some of the neighbors get together during the winter to play games. Mom always chooses Trivia—the silver-screen version." To her mother she said, "He's only here for a week, and even if he returned this winter, he wouldn't have time to play games."

"Your daughter's right about my schedule, Bess. Pretty demanding, but thanks for the compliment. One of my earliest teachers told me the best way to learn how to make a good film was by watching films—good, bad and in-between."

Bess pouted in a way that made Shane think she was portraying a character, not her true feelings. She sipped her coffee without comment then suddenly said, "He asked about your writing, Jenna."

"Hmm…"

"I was serious outside," Shane said. "About hiring you, I mean. If today is any indication of how much help Coop is going to be, I'm going to be stark raving nuts by the end of the week."

Jenna walked the rest of the way into the room. She still wasn't smiling. "I don't know how to write a script."

"I don't expect you to. That's my job. I need someone to bounce ideas off and give me feedback on characters. Make sure they talk and act like people who might live in Sentinel Pass. You know the local language. And the history. That's the kind of stuff viewers can relate to."

"Jenna," her mother exclaimed. "This is the opportunity you've been waiting for."

"It is?" Jenna looked from him to her mother and back. "I don't actually think screenwriting ever entered my mind as an aspiration, but thank you, anyway."

"Jenna Mae Murphy, I will disown you starting immediately if you don't take this job."

Jenna's lips twitched at her mother's theatrical threat. "Really? Does that mean I don't have to open the Mystery Spot this year? Because I really don't see how I can do both, Mom."

Her mother frowned. "Oh. I forgot about that. What if I work mornings, while you and Mr. Bernes—um, Shane, write?"

Jenna's mouth dropped open in obvious shock. "You? Lead tours?"

"Why not? I bowed out of active duty when you took over, but not because I forgot my lines." She cleared her throat and sat forward, back straight. "Step right up, dear guests, and explore the eeriest spot on the planet, where Earth's magnetic fields hold no power, and gravitational forces run contrary to accepted theory."

She sounded so much like an old-fashioned carnival barker, Shane clapped. "I can't wait for the full tour."

Bess smiled triumphantly. "See? I've still got it."

Jenna didn't look convinced, but he could tell she was running out of excuses. Spending every morning with her was a personal risk he was willing to take to save his butt where the show was concerned. And he'd insist she take the outrageously large salary he had in mind. A win-win, as Coop might say. But was it the right thing to do where his peace of mind was concerned?

He could only hope.

CHAPTER FIVE

"TELL ME YOU BROUGHT the talking stick," Jenna demanded of Libby the moment she appeared at her door.

"Hello to you, too. I had to go back for it, but I remembered," Libby said, handing Jenna a vase of bright yellow and purple tulips. "It's in the car. Here. Take this. My contribution to the book."

Jenna smiled. Leave it to Lib to remember the smallest detail, even when her life was gyrating in every different direction. This month's book for discussion was *Botany of Desire* by Michael Pollan. The second section of the book discussed how the cultivation of tulips had changed the map of the world.

"I'm impressed," Jenna said, her voice lifting as Libby had already dashed back to her vehicle. "When did you find time to cut flowers? I figured Cooper would want every spare moment of your time."

Libby, who was dressed in a pretty skirt of gauzy material and a teal T-shirt with a scalloped neckline, looked feminine and self-assured. The dark smudges that she'd been sporting under her eyes for the past couple of weeks were gone.

"He was so sweet. Waited on me hand and foot all day," she said hurrying up the steps. "We found the tulips at

Gran's. How'd your day go? When I dropped Coop at Mrs. Smith's house a few minutes ago, Shane said you showed him around."

Jenna closed the door behind Libby, glad to have a few moments alone before the others arrived. "Not exactly. He was at the Mystery Spot when I got there. I'll tell you all about what happened later, but guess what?" She reached out and touched Libby's arm. "I knew him in college."

"Seriously? Did you date?"

"No. Nothing like that. He was in one of my classes. He was ultracool—sort of the avant-garde artsy type—and I was a hick kid from the Hills. I thought he was intriguing. I may have fantasized about him, but I never went out with him."

Libby looked over her shoulder. "Where's your mom?"

"Upstairs. She's watching season two of *Deadwood* on DVD. Why?"

Libby lowered her voice. "Cooper was talking to Shane on the phone while I was getting dressed. I only heard Coop's side, but I got the impression your mother was one of the people Shane was interested in seeing test for a part. Did he tell you that?"

Jenna motioned Libby to follow her into the kitchen. "I need to chop chives for Kat's soup. She called earlier and said the deer ate hers."

"Poor Kat. She tries so hard but has the worst luck with gardens."

And life, Jenna thought, but didn't say so out loud. She certainly wasn't one to compare green thumbs, and her social life was even worse off. At least Kat had a couple to kids to show for her mistakes.

Jenna snipped a small bunch of shiny, fragrant reeds

from one of the small pots her mother kept on the window ledge above the kitchen sink. "By the way, she also said she's picking up Char, but they're running late."

"As usual," Libby said, not unkindly. They both knew how hectic their friend's life was. "So, tell me what Shane said about your mother."

Jenna worked carefully to avoid cutting herself. "He was very patient—even when she brought out her scrapbook. But you should have seen how intense he got when she told him about her dog idea."

"What dog—" The question was cut short by a knock. "Will you get that? I just need to finish—"

Libby was already on her way to the door.

Jenna was sorry she and Lib hadn't had more time alone. She didn't feel comfortable telling the others about Shane knowing in her college because she didn't want to answer any questions about why she dropped out of school.

"Hi, Jenna," Kat called, hurrying in with a loaf of bread under her chin and a slow cooker in her arms. "Sorry I'm late. Potato soup. No famine for this group," she said with a laugh. The cultivation of the potato and its impact on Ireland—and the world—was yet another section of the book.

Char Jones, fourth member of the group, shuffled into the room, wearing beaded moccasins that were easily two sizes too big. She had a plastic grocery bag over one wrist and was carrying a glass pie plate. Deep reddish-purple syrup glistened in a number of spots outside the golden crust. She slid the dish to the counter then hefted a six-pack of glass bottles to the counter. "Hi. It's my fault we're late, not Kat's. I forgot the beer. It's hemp. Kat bought it special, but I was storing it in my refrigerator and we drove off without it and had to go back."

Jenna spun around and burst out laughing. "Hemp. That's too funny. I wondered what you were going to do to get around the marijuana part of the book. Aren't you the clever one?"

Kat brightened at the praise, but she made a so-so gesture. "My partying days are so long ago and far away. And I even brought a root beer for Libby," she said, whipping out a bottle from the cloth book bag slung over one shoulder.

She twisted off the cap and offered it to Lib, who blushed a pretty shade of red.

Char, who had been busy opening the other bottles, passed them around, then held out hers to toast. "Kat told me the good news on the way over, Lib. Here's to a new baby in our midst. Life is interesting."

"Thank you, everyone. But that's only part of my news." She paused then grinning broadly added, "I—"

"Will tell you all about it after we eat and discuss the book," Jenna said, butting in. "You know this group, Libby. If we get off topic too early, we'll never get back to the book."

They all agreed with just a minor bit of grousing.

"Everybody grab a chair and sit. There's tea and some delicious-looking pie for dessert. What kind is it, Char? Did you bake it?" Jenna grabbed a ladle from the drawer and hustled her guests to the dining room table, which she'd set after Shane left.

Char hooted. "Are you insane? I don't cook. Zelma Broken Feather baked it. The filling is wild chokecherry. I was going to order apple because of the Johnny Apple-seed chapter, but then I tried a piece and couldn't resist.

And if you like it, it fits with next month's theme of eating local."

"Remind me what the next title is?"

"*Animal, Vegetable, Miracle* by Barbara Kingsolver."

"What's the date?" Kat asked. "I checked out the book from the library but haven't had time to read it."

Jenna tapped the neck of her beer bottle with her spoon. "Q and A next. First, a quick toast. Here's to Libby and Coop. Now, dig in while it's hot. We can talk about life stuff *after* we discuss the book."

They feasted, talked book and argued. Some were more impressed by the author's efforts than others. Libby had fallen in love with the author's writing and had already ordered another title of his from the Internet.

"It's called *The Omnivore's Dilemma*. If I like it, I'll probably suggest it when it's my month to host again."

"We've really been focusing on serious topics lately," Char said. "I'm tempted to change my choice, but I kinda like this food theme. Kat, the soup is delicious."

Kat beamed. "Thanks. It's my first mother-in-law's recipe. She used to say, 'Eat potatoes. Potatoes cheaper.'"

Everyone laughed, then Libby observed, "Jenna, I was sure you'd jump all over this book, but you've been freakishly quiet. Did you read it?"

Jenna pushed aside her mostly full bowl. Although she usually loved rich and creamy soups, her stomach felt like a small army had set up camp inside it. Maybe her mother's acid reflux was contagious. Or maybe her problem was due to the man with the serious brown eyes she couldn't stop thinking about. The man she not only found personally tempting, but who tempted her to put her business aside and follow a ridiculous old dream.

"I read it a month ago. I meant to skim through it again, but so much has been happening around here I ran out of time. Sorry."

"I assume you're talking about Cooper and the big to-do last night," Char said helping herself to another scoop of soup. "I can't believe I missed the meeting, but, boy, everybody who came into the store today has had something to say about what happened. No offense, Lib, but those Hollywood guys have some nerve assuming we're going to welcome them with open arms after what Cooper did to you."

Libby set her spoon down and looked at Jenna with a question in her eyes. *Now?*

Jenna waited for Char to finish eating then she pushed back her chair and stood. "If everyone is done, let's move into the living room. Libby, if you take the talking stick, I'll put the water on for tea. How are you doing for time, Kat?"

Kat tossed her blond ponytail and looked up as if thanking the heavens. "Both boys are with their respective fathers tonight, believe it or not. Whatever cosmic forces came together to save me the cost of a babysitter I don't know, but I sure do appreciate it. Finances have been tight lately. I even agreed to do henna tattoos during the bike rally. That's how desperate I am."

They'd all heard the story of how Kat wound up with unfortunate husband number two when she applied a henna tattoo of a serpent that wrapped around his back to his front. Nine months later after her second son was born, she vowed to give up the art. But she still operated a booth at craft fairs when money was tight.

"I understand," Jenna said, before heading into the

kitchen to fill the electric kettle. "With the Mystery Spot closed for two weeks, I'm going to have to make an extra effort to get bikers to come this way. Dad never believed in catering to one specific group, but things have changed since the Sturgis rally first started."

While the others discussed the social and financial impact of having thousands of motorcycle enthusiasts descend on the Hills for two short, intense weeks each summer, Jenna dropped tea bags in individual cups and sliced the pie. As she joined them, she spotted Libby checking her watch. Her friend was anxious to go. She had someone to go to. The realization left a bittersweet taste in Jenna's mouth.

"Okay," she said, clapping her hands. "Let's get the big announcement out of the way. Libby…"

Libby blushed but lifted her chin and said, "Cooper asked me to marry him and I said yes."

After three hugs and overlapping questions, Libby pounded the talking stick on the floor. "Let me answer, you guys." Her smile said she understood their excitement and surprise. "He wanted to talk last night after the meeting, but I was too wiped out. Gran had had a bad reaction to some new medication yesterday and…oh, it was so scary and sad." She took in a breath. "Thankfully, Cal was there. He seemed to know what to do to calm her, and was able to get her to bed. She's much better today. I took Cooper to see her and Gran remembered him." They could all see how much that meant to her.

She bit her lip as if embarrassed to say more but added, "Coop went down on one knee and asked Gran for my hand."

All three women heaved a collective, "Ohh."

"It was the sweetest thing I've ever seen. And Calvin offered to let us have the wedding in his garden. We hadn't talked specifics, then suddenly—" she snapped her fingers to make the point "—it was all decided."

"How soon?" Kat asked.

Libby swallowed. "This coming Saturday." She held up the talking stick. "I know. I know. That's fast. But…well, the fact that I'm pregnant is a big deal to Coop."

Char frowned. "For a guy who started out prepared to trade sperm for a share in a gold mine, he's really done an about-face. Are you sure about this, Lib?"

Libby nodded. "As sure as anything in my life. He's the one. And he can't wait to be a dad."

They'd all known about Libby's baby-by-contract scheme, and while each of them might have had their doubts, they'd tried to support their friend. Jenna was relieved things seemed to be working out so well, and she was sure Kat and Char felt the same, but still…Cooper was a stranger. Like Shane.

"We want to keep the ceremony simple. Coop says the faster we do this, the easier it will be to keep the press out of our hair. So, don't mention it to anyone, okay?"

"Who are you inviting?" Jenna asked.

"Just a few friends. You guys, of course, and Mac and Megan. Cooper's best friend, Shane. That's another reason to do it so quickly. Because Shane is already here. The only other person Cooper wants to invite is his neighbor, but he's not sure the guy can travel this far. He's Cal's age."

While the others talked wedding details, Jenna served tea and pie. She took the talking stick from Libby and pulled up a leather ottoman. "I have news, too. Not as interesting, but…" She made a face. "The Mystery Spot was broken into this morning."

"Oh, no," Kat cried. "Was there any damage?"

"A broken window and the hinge on one of the cabinets is screwed up. The deputy who came out figured it was probably a kid looking for something to steal. The damage might have been worse if Cooper's friend hadn't been there."

"What was he doing there?" Char asked, smacking her lips from the tangy flavor of the pie.

"I think he was scouting locations," Jenna said to avoid mentioning anything about college. "Anyway, the inspection went through without a hitch," she said, trying to work up the enthusiasm she knew she should be feeling. "We'll be open for business this weekend."

"What about the broken window?" Libby asked.

"Orton's Lumber had to order the glass, but they said they'd install it for free if they could post a sign in front of the Mystery Spot."

Libby smiled. "Everybody's jumping on the free publicity bandwagon, I see."

"Works for me," Jenna said. "I'm cash poor at the moment, although my other good news is Walt Gruen's daughter is back home and doing great, so he not only went out to the Spot this afternoon to backfill the trenches, but also volunteered to tack a piece of plywood over the broken window for me. Nice, huh?"

"The beauty of a small town where people care about each other," Libby said. "I wonder if the writers who work on the show will be able to get that across in their story lines. That's my only fear, you know. That they'll somehow turn us into a stereotype that isn't anything like the real Sentinel Pass."

Jenna hadn't thought of that. "Hmm," she said. "I've

been so wrapped up in Mystery Spot problems that never crossed my mind. Maybe I shouldn't have turned him down."

"Turned who down?" Kat asked.

"Coop's friend. The Bernese—I mean, Shane Reynard. I told you he gave me a ride home, and while he was here talking to Mom, he asked if I might be interested in helping him write the script for the pilot."

"Oh, my gosh," Kat exclaimed, nearly dropping her pie plate in her excitement. "That's fantastic. What a wonderful opportunity. When do you start?"

Jenna felt her cheeks heat up. "I told him I couldn't do it."

"Why?" Char croaked. "You're a talented writer. I read your poetry book."

"Poetry isn't dialogue. What do I know about scriptwriting?"

Libby sighed. "Cooper told me he'd put that bug in Shane's ear, so to speak. I got the impression you'd be more of an advisor than the actual writer, Jen. That's Shane's strong suit. According to Coop."

"Oh." Jenna set the talking stick aside. She felt foolish and embarrassed. She should have known she wasn't being asked to write. Her secret dream was just what her father called it—a waste of time.

"You're wrong, Libby," her mother's voice said from the staircase. "Hi, ladies. Didn't mean to eavesdrop, but the smell of chokecherry pie was too hard to resist. I bet Char brought it, didn't you, dear?"

Char jumped up to get Jenna's mother a piece as Bess strolled toward the group. "I'll take it upstairs with me. I know a lot of people were put off by *Deadwood*'s language, but the dialogue and character development is fantastic. Not contemporary, of course, but, oh my, the writers must have had fun working on that show."

Jenna looked apologetically at her friends, but no one seemed bothered by the intrusion.

"What did you mean when you said I wrong, Bess?" Libby asked.

"Will you join us?" Kat offered, scooting over on the couch to make room for her.

"I can't, dear. I have my show on Pause and don't want it to start up without me. But thank you." She smiled sweetly then looked at Libby. "While Jenna was on the phone with the plumber, I continued conversing with the handsome Bernese mountain dog." Jenna softly groaned. Her mother ignored her. "Shane told me that he felt Jenna's poetry was emblematic of her writing ability and he very much wanted to collaborate with her."

Before anyone could respond, Bess accepted Char's offering with a regal "Thank you so much," then turned and walked upstairs, like the classy professional she was.

Libby was the first to speak. "You have to take him up on the offer, Jenna. Not just for your sake but to safeguard Sentinel Pass's reputation."

"What reputation? Nobody's even heard of us."

"They will soon enough," Char said. "Especially after news of Cooper and Libby's wedding gets out. You know how people go gaga over that kind of stuff. The paparazzi used helicopters to crash Tom Cruise's wedding."

Libby blanched, but Jenna knew Char was right. "Mom actually volunteered to work mornings at the Mystery Spot," she said softly. Her friends were familiar enough with Bess's story to know what that meant.

"Wow," Kat cried. "This might be just the thing to get Bess involved in life again. Screw the town, Jenna, you need to do this for your mom."

Libby stood and walked to the phone. Since it wasn't a portable, she had to motion for Jenna to come to her. "Call Shane and tell him you accept. He and Coop are at Mrs. Smith's at the moment…wait…did Bess just call Shane a Burmese Mou—"

"Bernese mountain dog," Jenna corrected, rubbing her left temple in hopes of forgoing a headache. "It has to do with her idea for a character in the show. And, no, I've never seen one so I don't know if he resembles the breed or not."

Libby looked toward the stairs and smiled. "I'm going to do an Internet search when I get home. Does she have a breed in mind for Coop?"

"Golden retriever."

"*Ohh,*" she said with a wistful sigh. "She nailed that one. He retrieved me from the depths of despair." Her eyes were misty when she looked at each of them, then she glanced at her watch again. "I have to go. I'll call you all tomorrow with the details of the wedding. No gifts. Coop is catering everything."

She grabbed Jenna's hand and put the receiver in it. "Call him. Cooper is going to have his hands full this week with the wedding, and I know Shane is under some time constraints. That could be your wedding present to me, my friend."

Jenna wanted things to work out for Libby. Truly, she did. But the thought of working closely with Shane Reynard made her nervous. He knew about her past and he made her remember things she'd worked damn hard to forget. He was offering a chance to explore an aspect of her life she'd done her best to ignore. She knew what her father would have said about trying to make a living from her creative talents.

But Libby was proof that sometimes taking risks paid off.

"Okay. I will, but I need you to do something for me in return."

Libby hesitated. "What?"

"Tell me when we're going shopping to buy you a wedding dress, you goose. What were you planning to wear? Your postal shirt and jeans?"

Everyone laughed and the discussion shifted away from Jenna's situation. She would call Shane after her friends left, but she wasn't about to put the future of the Mystery Spot on the line. She might try working with Shane, but only if she could find someone to hold down the fort when she wasn't there. Luckily, she had just the person in mind, if she was still available.

"SO…WHAT'S A PREMISE again?"

Shane linked his fingers together and pushed them outward in a stretching mode to keep from wrapping them around his best friend's neck. Most people thought of Shane as a patient man, but working with Cooper Lindstrom would try Mother Theresa's saintlike qualities. "It's the underlying motivation that drives the story and makes viewers tune in each week to see what happens next. *Desperate Housewives* is about over-the-top dysfunction between families and friends in one campy neighborhood."

"I'd like our show to be more real."

Coop was straddling a chair at the kitchen table of the

house they'd rented. Despite opening every window to let in the warm breeze, the place smelled like somebody's grandma. Shane much preferred the scents of Jenna's house. It had reminded him of a library where he'd spent every free minute growing up. His secret place. Not-so-secret, perhaps, but not somewhere his brother enjoyed, so Shane had felt safe there.

"I agree. You're the hero. Flawed and needy but supposedly successful by most people's standards. What the world doesn't see is your broken side. The debt, the whack-job mother, the predatory she-bitch ex-wives…"

Coop made a face. "God, shoot me now. I didn't realize my life was so bad."

Shane patted his shoulder in support. "It sucks to be you—the character. We take the problems in your real life and make them a shade more *Desperate Housewives,* then we set you on a journey to find your truth and redemption."

"Libby."

"Sentinel Pass," Shane corrected. "Libby is the key that opens the door to your new world. Without her, you can't enter into the place that will ultimately be your salvation, but we can't make it too easy. Where would the *Lord of the Rings* be if Frodo got the golden ring in chapter one?"

Coop shrugged. "Point taken."

"So, although in real life, Libby fell in love with you from your e-mails. Our Libby—or the actor we hire to play her role—has to start out not liking you for very obvious reasons."

"Like what? What's not to like?"

Shane picked up his pencil. "You're shallow. Self-centered. Dependent on the attention of others. You have a group of sycophants who—"

"Sick what?"

"Groupies. Leeches. Your personal trainer. Your young, curvy assistant. Your slightly corrupt attorney. Your—"

"I get it. I get it."

Shane kept writing. "No. This is good. We can really develop a strong group of second-line characters who regard you as their livelihood. They aren't going to want you to outgrow your need for them. They'll fight to keep you in the dark, so to speak."

"They sound evil."

"They're not. They're human remoras. As long as you do what you do, they survive. Your job provides for them. They will do anything to keep you doing what you do."

Coop looked disturbed and anxious. "Okay, so we have the California people. What happens when I get to Sentinel Pass?"

"You have to deal with Libby's contingent."

"She has remoras, too?"

Shane pictured Jenna, who had appeared ready to stand up and fight for her friend. "Not exactly. These are her friends. Their interests aren't vested in her business, but they do have strong feelings about who messes with her. And there's the whole town to consider—fighting to keep its quiet kind of life. The trick is to make both sides human, not stereotypes. So your people will be acting on your behalf…mostly. And Libby's people will be acting on her behalf…mostly. But both sides want the status quo to remain unchanged. The only people who want change are you and Libby. And neither of you knows—or can admit— what you want to happen."

"Why?"

"I don't know. That's part of the backstory. Probably has

to do with your mother and Libby's dead parents or grand-mother."

"Did I tell you Gran remembered me?"

Shane ignored the question. "So once Libby finds out you're not being straight with her, she has to defend her town from your evil intentions. Here's the strong conflict that we build on every week. You're attracted to each other, but you're bad for each other so—"

"I'm evil, too?"

Shane got up and took two bottles of beer from the re-frigerator. He'd stocked up on food and drink at a little market in Johnson Siding after he'd left Jenna's. To his immense surprise, he'd found organic ginger ale and his favorite brand of snack chip on its shelves. He'd also picked up a package of South Dakota sunflower seeds that he couldn't wait to try. "In a self-serving, misguided schmuck kind of way," he said.

"I hate myself already."

"Good. Now we can start writing the script."

Coop opened the bottle and took a drink. "Shouldn't we have a team doing this? I've been to meetings on the lot. I've seen the rooms where the writers hang out. They have a big table—three or four times the size of this one. And a couple of those white boards with colored marking pens. Do you have any of those?"

"Not with me. But we have paper. And a couple of Sharpies. I bought those just for you."

Coop looked like a little boy who had just been told he was going to Great-aunt Edna's funeral instead of the zoo.

"Coop, we need to get words on paper. Just three twenty-minute stories. We'll keep these A-stories. Nor-mally, we'd include a B-story—something like Bess's dog lady and her relationship with say the guy who makes wooden sex toys—"

"Rufus makes Dream Houses."

"Not in *our* Sentinel Pass. You watch *Desperate Housewives*. Sex sells. And since we don't plan to let you and the postmaster have sex for at least two seasons, we need to have someone else doing it."

His friend's frown intensified. "If Libby and I don't have sex, how will you explain the baby?"

"No baby. Not right away. Lots of talk about a baby. In fact, at some point we want you to want the baby more than she does. That would be a great way to end season one. You could be standing in a department store looking at baby clothes and cry or something."

Coop brightened. "Cry? Like one tear, maybe. Nothing over the top. Yeah. I like that. Maybe we could go to the mall in Rapid City tomorrow and check it out."

"Or maybe…we could write these scripts."

Shane's tone must have conveyed his frustration because Coop winced. "I'm not much help, am I?"

"I didn't expect you to type the scripts in perfect form, Coop. I just need your input storywise. You started this and you're the heart and soul behind it."

Cooper didn't say anything for a minute. "What about Jenna? I thought you were going to ask her to help."

"I did. She said no…even with her mother pressuring her to do it. I'm not surprised, though, since I also came clean about knowing her in college. That wasn't a great time in her life, Coop. She's put it behind her and maybe I serve as a reminder."

"That sucks."

Shane agreed. "Plus, summer is her make-or-break time

at the Mystery Spot. When I left, she was organizing her staff to reopen on Saturday."

"But with what we'd pay, she could easily hire someone else to manage the place for her, couldn't she?"

"We didn't talk numbers. I got a sense that her writing is a private thing. Artists don't always get to the point where they're ready to share their work with the public."

Coop looked baffled. "But she published a book of poetry."

"Her mother's doing, remember?"

Coop frowned. "That's right. I could see my mother doing something like that…if I were a writer. Which I'm not. Are you sure you can't talk her into working for us? How 'bout if I ask Libby—"

The sound of a phone ringing saved Shane from having to make up some excuse why Libby shouldn't be enlisted to help persuade her friend to work for him. It was humiliating enough when Jenna turned him down the first time. Plus, after giving the idea some thought, he'd decided their working together was problematic, at best. What would he do if she started asking questions about his brother?

He got up and walked to the wall phone by the back door. *What's with these people?* he wondered. *Haven't they heard of portables?*

"Reynard here," he answered.

"Um…hi. It's Jenna. Murphy."

His pulse spiked. He looked at Coop and mouthed, "Jenna."

"Hello. How was your book-club meeting?"

"Good. It just finished. I, um, there's an extra piece of chokecherry pie left. I wondered if you'd like it. I could bring it over."

"Chokecherry?"

"It's a little red berry that grows wild along the river-banks in certain areas. It's good. It won't live up to its name, I promise."

"I know what it is. My mom used to buy chokecherry jam from a lady in the neighborhood. I just haven't heard the word in years." He looked at Coop. "But pie sounds great. If Libby has left, then Coop—" The sound of a chair screeching backward was quickly followed by a loud "Later," and a door slamming. "Is gone, too."

Jenna laughed as if picturing what had happened. The musical quality was as light and charming as any sound he'd ever heard and he was suddenly transported to that time in his life when he'd been young and filled with pos-sibilities and he'd fallen in love with a laughing girl with bright red hair and flashing green eyes.

"So," she said, breaking into his reverie, "I'll see you in a few minutes."

His hand trembled when he hung up the phone. His armpits tingled slightly, as if he'd had a close call driving his car. He walked back to the table and looked around, wondering what she'd think if she saw this mess. Loose-leaf paper scattered about. Coop's messy, illegible scribbles ac-companied by doodles and arrows only Coop could possibly interpret. Shane's notes—the few that there were—were squeezed together as if the price of paper was premium.

He left everything where it was. He wanted her to see what he was doing and how his creative process worked. Or, in this case, failed to work.

He took another swig of beer then poured the rest down the drain. So much for telling himself he didn't want to work with her. He did. Even if it was a bad idea.

He glanced at the table again and sighed. He'd make one last plea to enlist her help. If she turned him down, he'd call L.A. and hire a couple of screenwriters. Provided any were available on short notice and were willing to travel to South Dakota.

Normally, he'd hunker down on his lanai with plenty of ice water and his laptop. He probably could have pounded out a rough sketch of these scripts within a couple of days, but now, every time he sat down to write, his mind saw a girl with long red hair and a look of desolation in her eyes.

He didn't know if he was doing this for Jenna or for himself, but he was finally able to admit that she was the key. Over the years his memory of her had transformed into a shimmering image of perfection. Every woman he met paled by comparison. He'd put Jenna on a platform, then sealed her fate with a tragedy worthy of Shakespeare, his brother's actions making her even less attainable.

He wasn't sure how this was going to work, but he knew he'd never be able to move forward until he fixed the past. Maybe that meant coming clean about how he'd felt toward her, admitting that he'd had a crush on her. And because she'd left school so abruptly, his feelings had become frozen in time.

No doubt if they'd actually dated back in college, Shane would have discovered that Jenna was just another pretty girl, no deeper or more magical than any other girl he'd ever been attracted to. Working together now might be the reality check he needed.

CHAPTER SIX

"As you might have guessed, I'm here to apologize for being so abrupt today."

"I thought you were bringing me pie," Shane said, opening the door. He noticed Jenna's bike leaning up against a tree a few feet away. *No wonder I didn't hear her drive up.*

She held out a plastic-lidded container. "I did. I figured you'd have a fork. Mrs. Smith's son did leave all the household items behind after she died, didn't he?" She looked a little distressed. "I didn't even think to ask when I called to see about you renting this place."

He used his heel to hold the door as he took the dish from her. "No. I mean, yes. We have everything we need, and I talked to Mrs. Smith's son, Peter, on the phone last night. He said to make ourselves at home. Apparently, he and his sister are still at odds about whether or not to sell the house. They're in the process of getting it appraised so even if they put it on the market, we could probably stay another couple of weeks if we wanted."

"Good," she murmured, stepping inside.

She'd changed from the Mystery Spot uniform she'd had on that morning to cuffed white shorts with a black T-shirt. Clean lines. His favorite look. She'd left her hair down, just tucked behind her ears. She had nicely shaped ears, he noticed. Now would probably be the time to give her back the hair clip that was still in his pocket.

But he didn't.

"So," she said, turning to face him, "my, um, friendly neighborhood readers group told me I was out of my mind to turn down your offer, so I'd like to reconsider." She delivered the announcement in a rush of breath, as if she'd been practicing the line all the way over.

He closed the door and walked to the counter. He couldn't remember which drawer contained the flatware he and Coop had used earlier to eat the scrambled eggs he'd made them.

"That's great," he said, yanking open the most likely suspect. A great shifting of knives and spatulas clattered. "Wait. You do mean helping me with the scripts, right? Not shoveling dirt. Cooper told me there was no way in hell he was going to do manual labor when he needed to be planning a wedding." He paused. "Libby told you, right?"

"She made the announcement at our book club. We're all meeting in Rapid at noon tomorrow to help her pick out a wedding dress. Most of the time dresses have to be ordered, so unless something fits and they can overnight it… I don't know."

He tried another drawer. Yes. Gobs of mismatched forks and spoons. He grabbed a fork with the tines pretty evenly lined up then closed the drawer with his hip. "I take it her mother didn't leave behind—"

When she shook her head, her hair bounced in a lush wave that made his throat close up. He grabbed a bottle of water that he'd opened earlier before moving to the table. "Sit. Can I offer you, um, water? Beer?"

She pulled out a chair after glancing at the papers on the table. She didn't comment, but he sensed her interest. "No, thanks. I'm fine. Kat asked about an heirloom dress, but Libby said from the photos she has she thinks her mom wore a suit of some kind when her parents got married. My mom and dad, too. They eloped. I guess there was a big scandal."

"Why?"

"She was a student. Dad was fifteen years older and part of the faculty. He wasn't *her* teacher, but, still, he nearly lost his job." She made an offhand gesture. "Try the pie. Char bought it from a lady in Pine Ridge."

After nudging his notes out of the way, he pried off the plastic lid and inhaled. His mouth started watering. "Smells good."

He cut into the pointed end, making sure to get both top and bottom of the flaky golden crust with a thick, drippy dollop of berries. A long-forgotten, piquant flavor exploded in his mouth. He chewed and swallowed. "Wow. That is good. Tart but sweet."

She nodded in agreement. "So," she said a moment later, "after the girls left, Mom and I sat down and discussed schedules. I lucked out. Six of my students from last year still want to work, and one—Robyn—has been with us two summers. She's a very bright, gregarious person and she's interested in taking on more responsibility. Robyn and Mom will open, and I'll take the afternoon shift. I'll have to pay Robyn more, but depending on what you're offering…"

"Would ten thousand a week do?"

Her jaw dropped open. "Dollars?"

"Twelve, then."

"No. I didn't mean it that way." Her blush was so charming he almost choked on his pie. "You were kidding, right?" Twin spots of color on her cheeks deepened to a near chokecherry stain.

He coughed and made himself concentrate. Frowning, he gestured toward the table. "Take a look at how much Coop and I accomplished in three hours. If you hadn't called, there might have been blood."

She didn't look convinced.

He pressed his shoulder blades against the hard chair. "I'll e-mail my office and have my secretary send a list of recent contracts with writers for projects my production company has done. Salaries vary, but I think we can come to an equitable number—definitely enough to offset the cost of paying a manager."

She didn't say anything for a minute, but she did scoot closer to the table so she could see what he and Coop had been working on. "I don't even know where to begin."

He finished off his pie, then got up and walked to the sink to rinse the container. "Apparently, neither do I. I showed Coop the four outlines I'd been working on and he didn't like any of them." He looked over his shoulder and added, "By outline, I don't mean like a book with chapter headings and subpoints A, B and C. It's more of a *telling* version of the story that you want to *show* with the script you plan to write."

"Oh."

"Coop said my ideas were lacking any real connection to Sentinel Pass. He thought this house might be stifling our creative energy. He suggested using Libby's grandmother's cabin, but I told him I wanted a story, not a baby."

She smiled at that and the vessel he was holding slipped through his fingers. He juggled it gracelessly but managed not to drop it. Damn. How was he going to work with her when even a casual smile turned him into a giddy boy?

"Thank you for the pie. It was delicious," he said, carefully setting down the container. "If you don't mind my asking, where do you go when you want to write?"

When she didn't answer, he looked over his shoulder. She was reading his notes, using her finger to follow the small print with extra care. Braille was easier to read than his writing, his secretary often complained. But Jenna didn't seem to be having any trouble.

As he watched, a shiver passed down his spine as if she were actually touching him, not his words on paper.

He quickly dried the container using another paper towel, then carried it to her. "If you don't want to take me to your private writing place, maybe we could meet at the café in the morning. Grab a corner booth and you can tell me about the people who come in. Their history. How they're connected to Libby and the town."

She looked up. "These would be characters?"

"The nexus of a character." He found he was too restless to sit. Maybe he could keep his thoughts straight if he didn't actually look at her.

"The best stories are ones that people can relate to. *Everybody Loves Raymond* was a hit because even if you don't have an intrusive mother, you probably know somebody who does."

She frowned. "My father hated television and my mother preferred stage productions and movies, although for the past few months she's been ordering a lot of television series DVDs from NetFlix. When I was kid, though, I didn't watch much TV. Mostly, I read."

"Who was your favorite character from literature?"

"Honestly? Buck. From *Call of the Wild.*"

He stopped. "I would have guessed *Jane Eyre.* Or *Anne of Green Gables.* But maybe I shouldn't be surprised since your mother is such a dog lover."

Her snicker seemed to say she knew something he didn't, so he waited for her to correct him. "Mom isn't really all that much like the character she was telling you about. What name did you two decide on? Agatha? Aggie the dog lady? I like that, by the way. But I get what you're saying about real people with real stories."

"Real, but bigger, richer, campier, more over-the-top. Like the backwoodsman-slash-artist. And Aggie the dog lady, who may be considered past her prime but still has the same needs and desires of a younger woman."

Her lips compressed slightly. "You do know Mom's character isn't based on a real person, right?"

"They won't all be. We have room to have fun with this. Did you ever see *Friends?*"

She nodded. "When I lived with my aunt."

"Then you know that it was a comedy, but the writers tackled serious subjects—death, divorce, family issues. Once we establish our characters and premise, we can pull from real life and let these people get on with living. That's what will drive our show every week."

He waited for her to ask what a premise was. Instead she cocked her head slightly and said, "Is that what you and Coop were doing? Brainstorming the basics?"

"Yes. Although with Coop and me, it was a light squall at best."

She picked up her container and stood, but her grin was so real it made her eyes sparkle. This was an "old Jenna" smile—the kind he'd first fallen for back in college. His heart started thudding so loud he was certain she could hear it halfway across the room.

"So, since I have to run into town to look at dresses at noon, maybe we should save working at the Tidbiscuit for another day. Are you an early riser?"

"Yes."

"Can I pick you up at six?"

"Fine. Where are we going?"

"To the most beautiful writing spot in the world."

She said the words with such reverence he knew this was a place she'd never shared with anyone else. His pulse quickened and his fingertips tingled, but he did his best to remain cool and calm on the outside. "Great. I'll take any of the ideas we come up with in the morning and try to put together an outline. If you like it, we'll start plugging in some dialogue. I'm counting on you to tell me when I miss the mark. I mean that. A writing team requires trust and complete honesty and candor."

He wasn't sure how he managed to get those three words out without choking on them, but she nodded as if she agreed to his terms and was willing to give this her best shot.

"And if you give me your e-mail address, I'll have my secretary send you that information so you know I'm not taking advantage of you."

The weak overhead light made it hard to see her eyes, but she shook her head softly. "I never thought that. In fact, it occurred to me that you only offered me this job because you felt sorry for me."

The uncertainty in her voice made him close the distance between them. "Why would you think that? I drop into your world out of the blue and basically ask you to turn your life upside down. I'm the one who owes you, Jenna. Big time."

Her smile was very sweet, but it didn't jibe with the skeptical look in her eyes. "I wish I were as confident as you are that I'm going to be any help, but I'll try. That's all I can promise."

"I promise not to ask for anything more."

As he watched her ride away, he reached in his pocket and fingered the turquoise clip he'd unintentionally stolen. He rubbed his thumb back and forth across the smooth, polished surface of the stone. *This is going to work,* he thought. She could definitely write. He'd sensed raw talent in her poems. She wasn't afraid to draw from her gut. And she knew the area as well as anyone.

Yes, she was the one.

To work on this project. That was all.

He let go of the clip and closed the door with a bit more force than necessary. He needed to keep his mind on the job he'd hired her to complete. Jenna would benefit monetarily and on a personal level, too, he hoped. He still remembered the sense of accomplishment and wonder he'd felt the first time someone paid him for something he'd written—an article about a virgin surfer's first time on a board that came out in a regional travel magazine. That sale had changed his life—and how he thought about himself.

Maybe working on this project would open some doors for Jenna and help her remember a time when she had dreams she wasn't afraid to tell the world about.

JENNA PEDALED HOME slowly after leaving the Smith house. Her mind felt as if it were firing on all cylinders. So many ideas were bouncing around, she was sure if she closed her eyes and tried to sleep, she'd see a lightning show. She hadn't felt this fired up about the creative process since college.

College.

Shane wasn't the same guy she'd known in college. Not that she'd really *known* him exactly. But she had admired him from across the classroom. Drooled over him in daydreams. Unfortunately, in every version of her dreams she'd given him a complete makeover before introducing him to her parents. Clarence Murphy would have blown a gasket the moment he spotted Shane's earring, beard and ponytail. The pierced tongue and tattoo would have been nails in the coffin.

"Tattoo," she murmured, swerving to miss a pothole. She wondered if he still had it.

She'd never actually seen it, but the way his brother had described it had been one more reason why she'd chosen the prudent route and given her attention to his clean-cut twin that night.

"Shane went to the seediest part of Minneapolis and got the biggest, most garish, God-awful tattoo he could afford right in the middle of his back just to piss off our father," Adam had told her at the party.

She'd felt bad about snubbing Shane when earlier that week he'd actually said hi to her before class. A breakthrough, she'd thought, but then his Clarence-Murphy-pick-of-the-month, *almost*-look-alike brother had shown up.

Unfortunately, she'd quickly discovered that looks were the only thing the two brothers had in common. And by the time she figured that out, Shane was gone. To ease her disappointment, she'd kept drinking. Everything in her world changed after that...

She pumped her knees more forcefully to keep her mind off that particular train of thought. She hadn't revisited that night in years and didn't intend to now. What happened happened. There was nothing anyone could do to change that.

A loud honk made her jam on the brakes. Her rear tire skidded but she was able to come to a stop without losing control. She looked around and saw a large, familiar truck at the intersection. There wasn't a stop sign in either direction, but locals knew to approach the crossing with care because of the overgrown lilac bushes that blocked the view. If Mac hadn't slowed to a crawl, she probably would have creamed him.

Not that her bike was any match for his truck. She could have been badly hurt.

"Hi," she said, hopping off the bike and pushing it toward him. "Women drivers, huh? Sorry. My head was somewhere else."

His window was already rolled down, and he gestured toward the other side of the street. "Yeah. I think it would have landed in Mrs. Gate's strawberry patch if you'd run into me."

She laughed, but one part of her brain cried, *Oh. Nice line*.

"Well, thank you for being a safer driver than me. I was thinking about my new job. I signed on to help Cooper's friend write the first *Sentinel Passtime* screenplay."

He leaned closer to the window so she could see his face. Still one of the handsomest men she'd ever known—but for the first time that she could remember, her heart didn't make a funny little loop-the-loop when he smiled at her.

"I'm supposed to meet with the two of them sometime this week. They want to work out a deal to rent the mine when they start filming on location. The extra cash will be nice. Megan thinks we need a dog." He sighed and shook his head. "You heard about the wedding, huh?"

She nodded. "I'm going dress hunting with Libby tomorrow."

He frowned. "Everything's happening too fast, but nobody is listening to me. Even Gran seems happy about it. And Megan is dancing on the ceiling. We haven't told her about the baby yet, but Libby asked her to be part of the wedding party."

Jenna rose up on her toes to see if the little girl in question was asleep on the seat beside her dad. "Where is she?"

"Libby picked her up after she left your book-club meeting so they could look at flower-girl dresses online. I guess the wedding shop in town can get things shipped overnight from Denver."

Jenna hadn't known that. "Cool. Maybe Lib will find something, too. Did you work out an arrangement with Cooper where the mine is concerned?"

"Pretty much." He looked away, pretending to check the rearview mirror, even though Jenna could tell no one was coming. The night was still. Just the way the people of Sentinel Pass liked it.

When she looked at his face in profile, she felt a strange sensation—as if her perception had suddenly shifted and she was seeing him for the first time. A handsome hunk of a guy, but rough around the edges compared to a certain television producer. For years she'd told herself that if she ever fell in love, Mac would be the guy she'd want. But suddenly she knew that wasn't true. He was a friend. And that was all he'd ever be to her.

"Um…I'd better go," she said, feeling slightly light-headed. "It's getting dark and one close call was enough."

"Once the rest of the flatlanders get here, you probably won't be safe on the road."

She let her wave be her answer. But his prediction bothered her. She'd dropped out of college and moved home because she felt safe here. Did she really want to be instrumental in changing that aspect of her hometown?

A few minutes later she turned into her driveway. She put away her bike, then slipped in the back door. To her surprise, her mother was sitting at the table, her hands cupping a mug as if this were winter and she was cold.

"Hi. What's up? You feel okay?"

Bess blinked as if she'd been falling asleep—or deep in thought. "I'm fine. Decided to sip a little mint tea in case the pie aggravated my acid reflux, but, you know, I think it's better. I haven't had to take a pill in days. How'd the job interview go?"

Job interview? Not like any she could ever remember. "I start tomorrow."

Mom clapped. "Oh, good for you, Jenna. I'm so glad you got up the nerve to try. Don't worry. It'll be great. Bernese mountain dogs are wonderfully social and work well with others."

"Mom. You can drop the dog references. Shane said he likes your idea and is going to try to fit your character into the script. You don't have to keep calling him that."

"I can't help it. I have a feeling he's here to rescue you."

She looked so serious, Jenna wasn't sure what to say. "Rescue me from what? I'm doing fine. Better than fine. It sounds like he's going to pay me a lot of money to be a script consultant. That means we'll be able to do all those pesky fix-it jobs around the Mystery Spot we've been putting off." She looked at the peeling wallpaper behind the stove. "Maybe we can do a few home improvements around here, too."

When Mom didn't reply, Jenna looked at her. "What?"

"Nothing." Mom pretended to take a sip of tea. Jenna could tell the difference.

"Bessie," Jenna said trying to imitate her father's deep bass voice. "It's something. I can tell."

Her mother's sigh was large and theatrical, but also heartfelt. Jenna hurried to the table and sat. "What's wrong?"

"Today when I suggested selling the Mystery Spot, you acted like I was off my rocker. But the more I've been thinking about it, the more I have to wonder why we've never considered the possibility. This was your father's dream, not yours. And certainly not mine."

Her tone sounded almost as if she hated the place. "Mom, you gave up a career on stage to help Dad every summer. Can you honestly just walk away?"

"I think so. Yes. I'm sure I can. Maybe not last year, but I think Clarence would understand by now. The business was actually a point of contention throughout our marriage. I'm not proud to admit this, but there were many times I felt that that place meant more to him than we did. His family."

"You make the Mystery Spot sound like his mistress."

"It was. In a way. He could escape to it every day, and

he was certainly lord and master there. The only reason I didn't force him to choose between it and us was I wasn't certain which he'd pick."

Jenna got up and walked around the table to put an arm around her mother's shoulders. "How come you didn't mention this after Dad died?"

Her head touched Jenna's. "Because you stepped up and filled in for your dad so well. I thought running the place gave you purpose, and was good for your self-esteem."

Jenna pulled back. She walked to the sink to get a glass of water and give herself time to digest this odd revelation. She thought she'd been preserving her father's dream as well as working to keep a roof over their heads and help her mother. Instead, she'd been colluding with her father's mistress.

Wouldn't Shane like to get his hands on this? She pushed the thought away.

"It's probably too late in the season to sell the place, but—"

"I know that, Jenna. I didn't mean we should abandon the old girl, but new options are opening up and we need to be honest with each other, don't you think? We only have this one life to live. I don't have any regrets, but a few years from now I'd rather not look back and wish I'd taken my chance when it came my way. And the same goes for you, Jenna Mae."

Jenna understood what she what was saying. But what more did her mother want her to do? She was already risking public humiliation by sharing her meager and possibly laughable writing skills with a relative stranger. She'd agreed to hand over control of the Mystery Spot to a nineteen-year-old so she could spend time with a man who made her realize the supposed love of her life was merely her best friend's brother. Damn. She simply didn't think she could handle any more change at the moment.

"I'm really pooped, Mom. Can we talk about this in the morning?" She polished off her water and set the glass on the counter.

Her mother was watching her. "Of course. I told you Robyn's picking me up, right? She seems so excited about this promotion. She reminds me of you when you were that age—fearless in the face of any new challenge."

Fearless.

Maybe she had been. Once. Now...

"Mom, do you have any sleeping pills? I'm exhausted, but with so much on my mind, I have a feeling I won't be able to fall asleep." *Or stay asleep if my nightmare comes back.*

"Of course." Her mother stood and led the way up the stairs.

The benefit of a hypochondriac mother, Jenna thought, trudging after her, was having ready access to a vast pharmacopoeia.

CHAPTER SEVEN

SHANE WAS UP well before the appointed time to meet Jenna. His sleep had been restless and unproductive so greeting the dawn seemed as good a plan as any. He hadn't felt this unsettled in years, and he knew Jenna was to blame. She got to him. And it wasn't just guilt or some deluded sense of righting a wrong. She was like an itch he couldn't quite reach because it kept changing places.

He took the cup of coffee he'd brewed outside to the small, east-facing patio. Pale golden-pink threads of light were cutting through the misty fog that hovered in the tall trees beyond the yard. The sky was quite beautiful. It reminded him of growing up in Minnesota.

He muttered a low epithet and dropped into a wooden Adirondack chair after flipping over the pad to avoid the dew. Settling back, he kicked out his feet to the matching footrest.

One of his dreams had been about Jenna. They'd been holding hands, walking down a woodsy lane when his brother appeared from a converging path. He'd exerted some kind of Svengali charm over Jenna and she'd left with Adam before Shane could utter a word.

"It's not your fault, Shanely," Adam had called over his shoulder. "You can't help it if you're impotent."

"*Shanely,*" Shane muttered into his mug. The last time Adam had used the word, he'd converted it to an adverb.

"Don't act so damn smug and Shanely," Adam had shouted after their mother's funeral. "I was the full-time son. You're the one that got away. Distance creates the illusion of perfection. Every time Mom turned on the television, your name came up. 'I wonder how Shane is?'" he said in a mewling voice. "Every f-ing time."

Shane had wondered why Adam, who cursed like a gang member, had toned down his language, but when he looked over his shoulder and spotted the minister and their father, he'd understood. His brother was extremely conscious of maintaining his public persona.

The sound of a car pulling into the driveway scattered the memory. He rose and walked through the narrow breezeway between the house and garage. Two feet of the space was occupied by chopped wood, messily stacked.

The house had potential—in an HGTV way. Interior design was a hobby of his, but he wouldn't be here long enough to give the place a makeover. Heck, he'd be on a flight back home in a day or two if he didn't give the network execs a decent outline. Preferably by this afternoon.

"Hey. You're up," Jenna said, getting out of her Honda sedan. The faded yellow car bore the Mystery Spot logo on the door. Even from a distance he could tell the signage was a magnetic add-on.

What she really needed, he thought with a smile, was a new Volkswagen Bug with a hot-purple and yellow paint job. That would get people's attention.

"Coffee?" he asked.

When she shook her head, the sunlight, which had just

topped the trees, made her hair shimmer. As she came around the car, he saw she was wearing a short black skirt. Her legs were perfectly proportioned and athletic looking. This was a woman who exercised and took care of herself. She wore two tank tops, teal over pink. The pink showed a hint of feminine lace that made his mouth go dry.

"I brought along a thermos of sweet tea and some bakery cookies in case we get hungry. Grab whatever you need and hop in."

He had everything organized in his leather tote. He locked the door of the house—ignoring her bemused snicker—and joined her. Maybe locals left their houses unlocked but he was from L.A. and he sorely missed being able to punch in an alarm-system code before leaving.

"It smells amazing around here. Too bad there isn't a way to bottle that for the show," he said getting into the passenger seat. He reached down to release the catch so he could give himself more leg room. "Are you sure you don't want me to drive? Mine's bigger."

"Said like a true man," she said with a toss of her head. Before sitting down, she'd scraped back her hair in a ponytail held tight by a pink scrunchy. It reminded him that her clip was sitting on his bedside table.

He lowered his shades to look at her. "As opposed to a fake man?"

His tone must have held more of an edge than he'd intended because her pretty reddish eyebrow shot up. "Did someone not sleep well? Or are you not a morning person?"

"Yes and no. Where are you taking me?"

When she turned in the seat to back up the long driveway, her right hand brushed against his shoulder. The sensation set off a zing of awareness that penetrated his body armor of denial like a hollow-point bullet. *Crap.* The first time she'd accidentally bumped into him, he'd attributed his response to having been without sex for so long, but after the dream he'd had before dawn…nope. This was bad news. Apparently that college-boy-gotta-get-laid-or-die thing he'd felt for her years before was back. Or maybe it never went away.

Either way he was screwed. He was now her employer.

Script. Focus. The words sounded good, familiar, comforting, even. Then she started telling him about her favorite place on the planet. Her writing spot. And his palms started to sweat and his jeans felt too small.

"The lake is low right now," she was saying. "We really need rain. I don't suppose Hollywood could help us with that, huh?"

He shook his head. *Script. Focus.*

"But the view is very nice. And nobody goes to the spot where I'm taking you."

Alone. In the woods. On a beautiful morning with the woman of his dreams…who would carve his heart out of his chest with a dull spoon if she knew what he knew.

He clawed at the lever controls on the door to lower the window. The fresh, clean air he liked—still cool and moist—washed over him.

"Do you get car sick?"

Talk about emasculating… He shook his head. "Just absorbing the ambience." Lame. *Even Cooper writes better dialogue.* "Tell me the name of the lake again?"

"Pactola. It's a reservoir."

"Swimming? Boating? The usual?"

The prompt produced the desired effect—a chamber-ofcommerce-worthy spiel about the area. He listened with one part of his brain while reminding himself of how much he and Coop had riding on this. Especially Cooper. His best friend in the world. The brother he should have had.

Shane had worked in Hollywood long enough to know what happened when head writers got involved romantically with members of their staff. Not to mention the fact that only a self-absorbed idiot would begin a relationship on a lie. And if he told her the truth, he'd sure as hell never have a chance with her. Better to savor this time while he had the opportunity, because if he broke his vow to his mother and told her about Adam, that would end any connection they might have made. And he wasn't sure he could face the rest of his life without some kind of memory to sustain him.

Twenty minutes later they parked in a turnout that seemed made for her car, leaving behind the traffic of the highway. Not that there was a lot by California freeway standards, but they'd passed a steady stream of vacation vehicles, all shapes and sizes.

After a short walk along a barely detectable path that wasn't wide enough for two, they emerged at a spot that momentarily took his breath away. In the distance a blue jewel of a lake was surrounded by wooded hillsides. The only thing marring the perfection of the image was the several feet of bank exposed by the low water.

But apparently that didn't keep people away. A dozen boats rocked on ripples supplied by the ever-present breeze and a few active speedboats. Families congregated by the water's edge with a colorful tapestry of coolers, beach towels and shade tents. Fortunately, he and Jenna were far enough away to avoid the sounds of humanity. Their musical backdrop was the chatter of aspen leaves and bird calls.

"This is gorgeous. To get the clichés out of the way, do you come here often?"

She laughed as she pulled a quilted packing blanket from the backpack she'd been carrying. "A couple of times a week in the off-season. If I'm not subbing at the post office. Sometimes I sit and read. Or write in my journal. Nothing formal. Just scribbles. Observations about what's happening around me. Mom and I tend to get on each other's nerves if we're in the same house for too long, so this is a good break."

He sloughed off his shoulder strap and sat across from her. "Do you still write poetry?"

She kept her focus on setting out the snacks she'd brought. "A little. Um… You know I don't have much time. Wedding-dress shopping, remember? We'd better get started."

He opened his laptop and turned it on. "Shall I show you what little Coop and I sketched out? Then you can give me your gut feelings."

She folded her legs under her and rocked forward in an interested manner. He could read her curiosity and enthusiasm. It made him feel old and jaded by comparison.

He took a deep breath and closed his eyes, trying to focus on the premise of the show. "The first episode needs to set up the action. I thought we'd show Cooper some-one—we need a new name—and his to-be-determined sidekick sprinkling Coop's mother's ashes in the ocean while his secretary—as yet unnamed—delivers the news that he's broke and a bloodthirsty bookie is out to get him. Coop will probably be in his cups and grief stricken."

"He's okay with being portrayed as a boozer?"

"His *character* will have a lot of room for growth."

She threw back her head and laughed. "What a diplomatic way of saying you're making your best friend into a has-been lush with a mommy complex."

He chuckled, too. "Maybe that's why Coop was having trouble getting behind this."

They looked at each other and a sudden sense of awareness struck them both. Shane knew she felt it, too, because her fair skin suddenly turned pink and she looked at her hands. "What do you suggest?"

She cleared her throat. "Well, I like the idea of starting with the funeral, but what if we made his mother more of a Hollywood icon. A Liz Taylor type who couldn't bear to have a son more successful than her, so she subtly undermined his career. He might know this and feel a love-hate relationship?"

An image came into his mind. "Instead of a quiet tossing of ashes, there'd be a lavish Hollywood funeral. Maybe cameos from some legends or legend look-alikes." He hunched over typing furiously. "I like it. A lot. The studio would go nuts promoting it. Brilliant."

When he glanced up, he saw her blush had intensified.

He opened the screen further and scooted closer to give her a chance to see what he was writing. "Coop does the glad-handing. Exchanges barbs with his ex-wives. Wife?" He looked at Jenna.

Her bare shoulders lifted and fell.

She has great shoulders.

"The more the merrier, I guess," she said. "Because once he comes to Sentinel Pass, Libby's friends are going to use all of these social gaffs as fuel to keep Libby and Cooper apart."

He nodded, impressed by her ability to think ahead. "Good. Coop can help with this dialogue. He has plenty of experience where his exes are concerned." He typed in the basic setting, a few hints of stage direction: black hearse heads line of expensive cars, limos and Hummers. Luminaries, dignitaries, stars and starlets. Coop stands out, his gofers hovering.

"Coop needs a crew. Sycophants. Users with some marginal job."

She pursed her lips. "I can see that. They'll be the ones pulling him back when he tries to move forward, right?"

"Exactly. Any ideas?"

She pulled a notebook from her pack. "Well, I was thinking about this after I left you last night. My strong point is probably going to be the Sentinel Pass characters, but the day I picked up Libby and Coop after their hike, Coop muttered something about firing his trainer."

Shane flashed the thumbs-up sign. "Good one. We'll call him Guy Gillespie—trainer to the stars. Or, in this case, *star*. Singular."

She looked pleased with his response. "I don't know why, but I sort of pictured him as a young Jack LaLanne wannabe. You know who I mean, right? Jack LaLanne was a hero of my father's because he combined celebrity and healthy living. Dad said the guy once towed a string of boats from Alcatraz while handcuffed…or something. Our guy might try to replicate that kind of thing—like towing a party barge across the Great Salt Lake—but fails."

Shane could see it. Clearly. "So, he talks big while training Cooper. Always planning his next feat. Damn. That's brilliant. Quirky. Very Hollywood. I know an actor who could pull this off without trying. Excellent idea. Anything else?"

She consulted her notebook. "Um…maybe a lawyer who talks really fast so nobody understands anything he says."

"Like it. He might have been Coop's mother's lover many years ago. Maybe he thinks he's Cooper's biological father, but the mom would never let Cooper be tested because the not knowing kept other doors open."

She looked at him, frowning. "That's not really true, is it? I mean where Coop is concerned."

He finished typing before answering. "No. Lena Lindstrom was too ambitious for that. Coop's father was probably a studio mogul, but most of those players are dead now, so he'll never know for sure. Which is not necessarily a bad thing," he added without intending to.

"What do you mean? How can not knowing who your father is be good?" Her tone sounded slightly offended.

"I was speaking for myself. My father and I had zero in common. When I was a teenager, he told my mother that he was sure I was gay. This was a good thing because it let him off the hook—parentingwise."

"Why?"

"You know. The nature/nurture debate. He was on the side of nature. In this case. In everything else, he was in big business's pocket."

"You didn't like him much."

"Did you like your father?"

"Yes. He was brilliant and opinionated, but so darn smart you had to listen even if you disagreed with what he was saying."

"And if you did disagree, would he listen to your argument?"

She nodded but took a few moments before saying, "If

I provided corroborating evidence. He was too much of a scientist to ignore another opinion out of hand, but he wouldn't hesitate to blow your argument out of the water if you were in the wrong."

Interesting, Shane thought, recalling that she'd implied earlier that her father didn't champion the arts in any way. "What would he have thought of what we're doing?"

Her shoulders sank slightly. "Well, he probably would have supported me because of the potential increased tourism, but I doubt if he would have actually watched an episode of the show—whether I helped write it or not."

Shane nodded. "Ah, yes, you said he hated television."

"Because it dumbed-down the children watching it, in his opinion. That's why he poured so much of his time and resources into the Mystery Spot. He used to say, 'If just one child who comes here becomes intrigued by what he sees and goes on to study science, I've done what I was set on this planet to accomplish.'"

He typed a few key words: mad scientist, passion for the masses, quirky, beautiful daughter carrying on father's dream.

When he looked up, she was staring at him. Her lips were pursed in a serious but sexy way. His throat went dry and he could no longer feel the keypad under his fingers.

"Even though Dad published a dozen treatises and highly respected position papers within his field, he felt fiction—storytelling—was a waste of time. He didn't speak to my mother for a month after she had my poetry published. He called it a waste of paper."

Shane almost deleted what he'd typed. Maybe he didn't want to immortalize this guy. "Did he read it?"

She shook his head. "I don't think so. If he did, he

didn't tell me. Or Mom. But I understood." She looked at him as if reading his doubt. "Really. He was a man of science who tried to share his passion with the world. That's why I'll never sell the Mystery Spot, even if Mom is ready to call it quits. I owe him that."

He started to ask why but changed his mind. Who was he to question one's sense of obligation to a parent? His promise to his mother was the reason he was here.

"How would you feel about bringing his character to life and creating a quirky tourist trap for the show? We'd have to rename it. The Mystery Zone…or maybe the Oh-Zone. *Oh*. Get it?" He typed and angled the screen for her to see.

"Cute."

Her smile sent a rush of tingles all the way to his toes. Heat stroke? Heart attack? Gout? He forced his brain back on task. "This guy could serve several purposes. He might teach science during the year then devote his time to the business every summer. A quirky bachelor. Maybe a love interest for your mother's character—Aggie the dog lady. I guarantee the attention would be good for business."

"Won't people consider that a little self-serving or a conflict of interest?"

His laugh was the one Coop called "sninical"—a combination of snide and cynical. "Probably, but since I'm the producer, I can do what I want—within reason and good taste—as long as the dozen or so studio honchos and their sponsors agree." She looked daunted. "But if I explain that we can spin this character as a way to spoon-feed a little science to the masses, I'm sure they'll approve."

The way she was worrying her bottom lip told him she wasn't sold on the concept, so he reached out to reassure her.

That was all. Just a little pat on the arm. Her bare arm. Where the sun had warmed the soft, smooth skin to a velvet texture.

"I'll play with him. Not too over the top, but if he blows things up from time to time, we might get some good visuals." His thumb stroked a slow, deliberate circle above the inside of her wrist. He couldn't miss the surge in tempo of her pulse.

She pulled away and began stuffing things into her backpack. "We should go. I don't want to miss helping Libby pick out her dress."

He checked his watch. She had plenty of time. This was her way of telling him he'd crossed the line. He understood, but her reaction hurt. More than it should have. He was her boss. He had no business flirting with her. Or touching her. He knew that. But deep down there were still traces of that troubled young man who'd been too unsure of himself to do more than admire her from afar. That kid *invented* sninical. *I told you, man. She's out of your league. Now, you know what would have happened if you'd asked her out in college. She'd have shot you down.*

"WELL, YOU JUST TELL Mr. Slobbering Pooch to stay the hell away from me," Char said on a growl. "My story is not up for grabs."

Jenna had arrived at the bridal boutique on Main fifteen minutes early, but she'd found her friends already there, gathered in the rear of the building surrounded by walls of white gowns. Voluminous designs of satin, lace, organza and beads.

After the disturbingly intimate work session with Shane—what had she been thinking taking him to her most private retreat in the world?—Jenna had to fight to keep her attention on the business of picking out a dress. She'd probably made a mistake by mentioning that Shane planned to give his Libby character friends, like them.

"Nobody would be interested in my story," Kat said, looking up from the circular rack of discounted designs she'd been poking through. "And I'd be darn surprised if he drooled, Char. Even in his sleep. Like my first ex-husband did. I put a saucer beside Pete's pillow once to prove it. He was furious the next morning. No wonder we divorced."

Jenna, who had her notebook clamped under one arm and a pen between her teeth, held up a gown that felt as if it weighed thirty pounds. "'Is one?"

Both women made faces that basically said, "Good Lord, no."

She shoved it back on the rack and took the pen from her mouth. "Shane wouldn't use your life story per se, Char, just bits and pieces of it. We talked about turning Rufus into a backwoods artist who blushes when a woman talks to him but carves slightly lewd masterpieces using a chain saw."

Her two friends looked at each other…and laughed.

"What's so funny?" another voice asked. "Not my dress, I hope. I like this one."

Jenna turned as Libby walked toward a large mirror suspended between racks. "It's gorgeous," she exclaimed swallowing a large lump in her throat. "You look like a princess."

"We call this day length," Gretchen, the fiftysomething clerk who was helping them, said, offering Libby a hand up the two-step platform so everyone could see the hemline from all angles.

"I love it," Kat exclaimed, rushing closer.

Char pulled out her camera and snapped a couple of shots. "It's smart, not overly fussy. It's you, Lib."

Libby shoved her hair back from her eyes. She looked at them seriously. "Do you really think so? This is the first one I tried on. Are you supposed to choose the first one you look at?"

"If you're getting married in three days, yes," the ever-practical Kat said. "Besides, it's perfect."

Libby twirled around again, her hands settling on her hips. "It's pretty, isn't it? And the best part is it fits. In fact, the lace is sort of stretchy. I don't know how they do that, but it's very comfortable."

"Will you be wearing your hair up or down?" Gretchen asked, walking up with two different styles of veils in her hands.

Libby looked at Jenna. "Um…up?"

Jenna checked with Kat and Char. One nodded and one shook her head. A split vote.

"Up," Libby declared. "And no veil. It's just not me."

The woman dropped the gauzy material over the back of a chair. "What about a small, classy tiara?"

"Oooh," Char said with childlike enthusiasm. "A tiara. Every woman should have one. You could borrow mine, but it's not small or classy. In fact, it's silly and gaudy, but I love it."

Jenna and Libby looked at each other in the mirror. *Who knew,* they mouthed.

Jenna reached for the notebook she'd set beside a thick album featuring men's tuxedo choices. Shane would love this dialogue, she thought—even if he wouldn't have used pen and paper to record it.

She clicked the tip of her pen and quickly jotted down the image and a few words of dialogue. Last night, when she'd reviewed Shane's and Cooper's notes on the table, she'd assumed that was how he worked. But this morning, when he'd pulled out his laptop, she'd felt pure panic. She was a pen-and-paper kind of girl. Her mind needed the longhand connection to flip that creative switch in her brain. Didn't it?

Half listening to her friends' chatter, she wondered if she was kidding herself. Of course *real* writers composed on computers. They couldn't afford to waste time transferring notes from one medium to another.

She flicked the top of the pen and tossed it in her purse. Tangible proof that her writing skills were just a hobby. Poor Shane would figure out soon enough that she wasn't up to the high production demands of Hollywood.

"Cooper would like this one," Libby said firmly. "Don't you think so, Jenna?"

Jenna looked up. "Delicate and ladylike. Very nice," she said.

Libby adjusted the sparkly crown a little and sighed. "He thinks I'm both of those. Isn't he funny?"

Jenna felt a brief second of envy. Would anyone ever think of her that way?

"No. He's intuitive and smart." She walked to Libby and gave her a quick hug. "So, our work here is done, right? On Saturday you are going to be the most beautiful bride on the planet and the rest of us can wear anything we want."

"Absolutely. Think of this as a garden party. Pick something colorful and fun."

Jenna had just the dress. One her mother had bought a

year ago when a friend, who ran a vintage clothing boutique, sold out to move to Arizona. She looked down at her durable, thick rubber-soled hiking sandals. *I could use a new pair of shoes, though.*

"Shoes," she exclaimed. "Lib, what you going to wear on your feet?"

Libby's eyes twinkled with a hint of tears. "I'm going barefoot. Gran suggested it, and Cooper thought it was a great idea given our history."

"What history is that?"

Libby's cheeks turned rosy. "Never mind. I… I'm going to take this off. Don't you have to be at the Mystery Spot about now, Jenna Mae?"

Jenna checked her watch. "Oh, crap, I have to run. Sorry to miss lunch, you guys. Eat something fattening for me. Lib, I love the dress. Perfect choice. I'll talk to you later."

As she hurried to her car, which was parked midway between the bridal shop and the ten-story Alex Johnson Hotel, she noticed a stretch limo double-parked at the corner of Sixth and St. Joe, near the statue of George Washington. She tensed. Some Hollywood executive already? Shane hadn't mentioned anything.

She paused to watch as the driver opened the rear door. A man got out. Tall. Black sunglasses. Expensive-looking dark suit cleverly disguising the fact that he was carrying a bit too much weight around his middle. His close-trimmed beard and mustache, which sported a hint of silver, masked thick jowls, but he moved adroitly, disappearing into the hotel without sparing a glance at the statue.

She let out the breath she'd been holding. She hadn't been able to get a good look at him, but she'd bet money that he wasn't from California. He looked too intense, but there was something familiar…

Before she could puzzle any more on the subject, someone called her name. Kat came rushing toward her with Libby's cell phone in her hand. "Oh, good, I caught you. Shane is on the phone and he wants to…here. You talk to him."

Jenna held the phone to her ear. "Hello?"

"Jenna? Great. Libby didn't think they'd be able to catch you. Hey, listen…if it's not a problem, I'd like to meet you at the Mystery Spot this afternoon. I've been playing with the idea we talked about…the Oh-Zone. I'd like to run what I've got by you while it's fresh."

She was dying to ask for details, but she didn't want to keep Kat waiting. "Sure. You know the way. The glass guy is supposed to be there. Maybe you can make sure he does the job right."

"My pleasure. See you in an hour or so."

My pleasure. She knew the casual rejoinder didn't mean anything, but she couldn't stop the sudden flush she felt creeping into her face. She'd been experiencing odd little hot flashes—too localized to be the kind her mother complained about—ever since he'd touched her arm that morning.

"Everything okay?" Kat asked, studying her too closely for comfort.

"Yeah," Jenna said, handing her the phone. "He has an idea he wants to run by me. I guess he was inspired by something I said."

"I'm not surprised. You're the most creative person I know. He's really lucky to be working with you."

Jenna went still. "Do you mean that?"

Kat nodded. "I wouldn't say it if I didn't."

Jenna wasn't sure that was true. Kat was the sweetest, most caring person Jenna had ever met. She had a big heart and she seldom rocked the proverbial boat—even when her ex-husbands deserved a good dunking. But the praise felt good. Especially since she felt so far out of her league.

"Well, um, thanks. I appreciate the vote of confidence. I'd better go."

"If we see any dresses we think would look good on you, do you want us to put them on hold?"

"No, thanks. I'm going to wear the one my Mom bought from Fillerie's. Remember it?" She'd never worn the pretty, totally impractical dress, but she'd shown it to her book-club friends as proof of Bess's inability to stick to a budget.

Kat's eyes went wide. "I do. It'll be perfect."

"I don't know if it fits," Jenna admitted, sheepishly, re-membering how angry she'd been with her mother for buying it. Later she'd told her friends that she was afraid she was turning into a less-well-educated version of her father.

"I wish I had a pretty dress hidden away in my closet," Kat said with a sigh. "Maybe if I wish real hard, the dress fairy will stop by my house tonight."

"If I was twenty pounds lighter…"

Kat hugged her quickly. "You mean if I was six inches taller. Don't worry. I have something I think will work. See you later."

"Bye."

Jenna watched her friend walk away. Kat's financial struggles were even more complicated than Jenna's because she also had two children to feed. All Jenna had to worry about was a business that barely broke even. But now, thanks to the income Shane had promised, she didn't have to worry about that.

As she headed out of town, she thought about the documents Shane's secretary had e-mailed to Jenna that morning. The money to be made in the entertainment industry defied logic and perspective. Even if Jenna asked to be paid the going rate at the bottom rung of the screenwriters' pay scale, she'd make enough in a few weeks to pave the parking lot and buy an alarm system.

Did that mean she was ready to sell out and move to Hollywood? Not hardly. She'd gladly take the money Shane was offering, but she wasn't ready to give up on her father's dream—or trade it for her own.

Keeping the Mystery Spot open was the only way she knew to prove to her father that she wasn't a failure. Which, she had to admit, was probably too pathetic for words, since her father was dead.

CHAPTER EIGHT

"ARE YOU SERIOUS about using my mother?"

Shane was washing windows. On a ladder outside the very window he'd nearly killed himself looking in the day before. The irony wasn't lost on him.

He could hear Jenna perfectly, even though she was inside the building, rubbing off the smudges the repairman had left on her new glass. Shane pointed out a spot she'd missed. He was doing manual labor because Jenna had insisted she wouldn't be free to work on the screenplay until everyone was gone.

"Depends on her screen test. Not all stage actors transfer to the screen. And vice versa."

She rubbed furiously. "A screen test? Where? Are you bringing in a film crew? When?"

He shook his head. He could have gone into detail about just how complicated and how many insanely trivial and petty hoops you had to clear before you ever saw a green light to begin production, but he didn't want to scare her. "She'll have to go there. The studio has a big stake in casting and they take an active interest. I should be there, but my assistant can e-mail me the footage. Unfortunately, we can't pick a cast until the actors have something to read."

She gave the corners one last rub then stepped back to

survey her work. "Nice. Double pane. Looks good. I wish I could afford to replace them all."

"You can…if our show gets picked up."

She set the cleaning products back in the bucket she'd been carrying around since he arrived and walked outside. He tucked the corner of his rag in his hip pocket and backed down the rungs of the ladder. "Hey, you do good work," she said. "Writer. Producer. Window washer."

He handed her the spray bottle. "Nice to have a trade to fall back on," he said lightly.

"That's what my father said about a college degree."

Her voice held that hollow sound he sometimes heard when she mentioned her father. "I never went back, either," he said. "I think I have about eight units left. Terrible, huh? My mother bugged me about it for a couple of years but finally gave up."

"Couldn't you have transferred to California?"

"Probably, but money was scarce and I was working full-time and then some. A man I respect told me the best way to learn a trade was from the bottom up. So, that's where I started."

"Is that when you met Coop?" she asked as they headed to her little office.

"A few years later. By then I had my SAG card. I got my start as a stunt double in a few low-budget films. Talk about crazy. At night, I'd ice down my bruises and try to write screenplays. The first one was so bad Coop and I burned it in our hibachi the first year we lived together."

She stopped suddenly. "You torched your work?"

"Yeah. Because it stunk. Literally. Not only was the writing atrocious, my roommate at the time was an unemployed pothead and a chain-smoker. The place reeked."

She unlocked a supply cabinet that was cleverly concealed in the siding. This was the second such hidden nook he'd stumbled across since his return to the Mystery Spot. He was beginning to get a feel for Jenna's dad. The guy didn't believe in wasting anything—not mismatched trim or space.

She stored the bucket and cleaning products on a shelf that had been made from an old billboard. The wood was slightly warped, and peeling paint was still visible.

After locking up again, she looked at him. "I've been thinking about your idea for the Oh-Zone. I like it. A lot. But just how kooky would we have to make the owner? I wouldn't want anyone to think I was making fun of my dad."

Shane stepped back to give her room to lead the way to their next task. "You have a thing about all those everyones and anyones, don't you?" He tried to keep his tone light so she wouldn't take his comment as a criticism, but she did anyway.

"Yes. I care what people think. I will be living here long after your film crew is gone. Long, long after this show has its run. I don't want to walk down the street and have people whisper, 'There's the girl…woman…old lady who turned her father into a laughingstock.'"

God, he loved her fire and passion. He'd give anything to be able to feel that passion turned to lovemaking. Had she been with a man since the rape? The question was wrong on so many levels he had to turn and walk away to regain some focus. "Where are you going?"

"Back to the Dizzy House. Maybe if I had a tour of the place, I'd understand what your father was trying to do here."

"Oh." She followed a few steps behind. "Why didn't I think of that?"

Because you weren't desperately trying to avoid thinking about sex.

"Shall I give you the whole spiel?" Jenna asked, hurrying to catch up—in more ways than one. Something had happened a moment earlier. She'd felt an electricity between them. A snap and spark that was undoubtedly sexual, but he'd turned it off as if he'd just learned she was an ax murderer.

She wanted to ask why but decided to play it safe. If she didn't ask, she wouldn't have to deal with the fact he hated redheads or something.

"Sure," he answered. He stopped at the wide concrete steps that led to the door. Above the transom was the sign her father had burned in wood when she was a kid: Watch Your Step. He'd meant that literally and always warned parents to hold their child's hand securely.

She trotted past him and opened the door, then turned to face him. "Ladies and gentlemen, please heed this sign." She pointed upward. "You are about to enter a building that to the naked eye looks very ordinary. The house was built in the 1950s after the original farmhouse that sat on this spot burned down." She leaned forward and pointed to the moss-covered rocks in the wall. "Notice that this building rests atop the exact foundation of the first home. When my father bought this property and first experienced the anomalies you're about to see and feel, he researched the history of the land. Inside you'll see excerpts from a journal written by the matriarch of the family who settled here in the late 1800s."

She cleared her throat and looked at him. "Can I give you the short version from now on?"

"As long as I get my money's worth."

She rolled her eyes. "Each tour accommodates ten to twelve people. A dozen adults in here is a pretty tight fit, but most families come with kids. Usually, the children push to the front of the pack, so I direct my talk to them."

"Why?"

She smiled. "You'll see. First I give people a few minutes to read what's in the glass cases on the wall. All six are the same excerpt, by the way."

"Are they real?"

She cocked her head and watched him read. "What do you think?"

He didn't answer right away. In fact, he stepped closer and traced the loopy scribbles on the glass—just as she'd seen hundreds of tourists do. "Looks real."

"The purpose of the journal is to plant in your mind a seed of doubt. Could this be more than just a trick? Could something phenomenal be taking place right under your feet? A hundred-year-old scientific anomaly, perhaps?"

He turned to face her. "You tell me."

The seriousness in his tone made her step back. "Um, well…decide for yourself. After my initial introduction and a few minutes to read the journal, I draw their attention to the room on the right. The kitchen." She stepped through the opening but gestured for him to remain where he was. "I need a volunteer."

With a smirk that she was beginning to find rather endearing, he raised his hand. "Me. Me. Pick me."

A crazy jolt of something she really didn't want to think about made it hard for her to answer with similar humor, but she tried. "Um…you, sir. In black." Motioning him forward, she added, "Normally, I choose a woman for this demonstration, but I don't want to be accused of being sexist."

His low chuckle as he followed her to the antique stove was too intimate, too interesting. When she looked at him, their gazes met and neither looked away for more seconds than seemed right. The words she'd recited several thousand times left her.

"Am I supposed to be dizzy?" he asked.

She moved back slightly. "Not yet. This is the egg trick. Well, it started out as the egg trick, but people accused Dad of using loaded eggs. Plus, they got expensive, so he switched to cue balls."

She opened a drawer and withdrew one and a half cue balls. "Before and after?" he asked, handing them back to her after he'd thoroughly examined both.

She smiled. "Just trying to prove that our cue ball is the real deal."

Clearing her throat, she resumed her spiel. "Can you imagine how annoying it must have been to the woman of this house to set a farm-fresh egg on the counter only to watch it roll off? Every time."

She demonstrated. The counter not only looked completely level, her father had rigged a large builder's level to prove that the fluid bubble was right where it was supposed to be. But when she set the ball on a purple spot it rolled to the right. A net had been tacked to the side of the counter to catch it.

"Your turn," she said, giving the ball back to Shane.

His right eyebrow shot up, but he did as asked. "There must be a magnet somewhere," he said. "Under the counter."

She opened the cupboard doors. Empty.

She was a little surprised when he got on his knees to look up under the counter, but maybe the fact he had some training in carpentry made him more curious than she'd expected.

He investigated thoroughly, repeated the trick several more times then looked at her and said, "I give up."

She put the two balls back in the drawer. "Then our work here is done. Come along. Next room."

He grabbed her hand as she started to leave. "Aren't you going to tell me how it's done?"

His hand was large and warm. Normally, she didn't like to be touched. Especially by men with large, warm hands. But her usual repulsion didn't happen. Instead she was tempted to squeeze his hand and hold on tight.

Bizarre, she thought, pulling her fingers free. "Gravity."

His chuckle followed her as she hurried to the doorway of the adjacent room. He walked to the waist-high cased opening that allowed people to observe anyone who entered the large, mostly empty room. Her father had hired an artist to paint murals on each of the outer walls showing what the room might have looked like when a family had lived here. There'd been many a day when Jenna had wished she could go back in time and live in this safe, pretty room.

"As you can see, this was the bedroom. We've removed the furniture to avoid injury, but imagine what a nightmare it must have been to sleep in a room that seems to be constantly shifting from side to side. We call this the dizzy room for a reason, so don't be surprised if a stranger is suddenly holding on to you for balance."

She took a deep breath and walked straight to the middle of room. Almost instantly, her equilibrium went haywire. She stepped on what looked like a level surface and felt her foot drop a quarter of an inch. Just enough to throw her balance off. She staggered, which prompted Shane to dash into the room.

"Watch out," she warned.

He weaved to the left like a drunk after a long night at a bar. "Holy crap," he muttered. "What the he—?"

She grabbed his arm and pulled him closer to the wall. He looked slightly dazed. "Wow. What is it?"

"You'd have to ask my dad. Unfortunately, I think the secret went to the grave with him. All I know is it's very effective. I've seen people bob and weave all the way back to their car. I've done this tour so often I barely feel it unless I'm in the middle of the room."

He put a hand to his forehead. "I've got the spinners. Like those nights in college when you drank too much then lay down in bed and the ceiling was going around in circles."

College.

He looked at her so intensely she realized she must have said the word aloud.

"Sorry. Wrong thing to say."

She shook her head. "It was a long time ago. Shall we finish the tour? There's an exit through the back, but since I have to lock up, I think we should go out the way we came in."

His usual serious look was back on his face. He nodded and pushed off from the wall to lead the way. He only made it a few steps before listing sideways, like the *Titanic* after meeting the iceberg. She tried to keep him upright, but his momentum was too great. They both staggered a few steps then crashed into the wall. The wall with the drawing of a four-poster with a patchwork quilt on it, and they landed smack dab in the middle of the one-dimensional mattress.

"This was your plan along, right?" Shane asked, wrapping his arms around her to keep steady. "To get me in bed?"

She laughed to keep her panic at bay, but to her surprise she didn't feel the usual fear that came when someone got too close, too fast. In fact, she liked the feeling of being in his arms. Warm. Secure. Protected.

"I've seen the same thing happen to other people. Perfect strangers. Dad used to say it was all about a person's polarity—positive and negative."

His eyes were such a deep, yummy brown. Like chocolate syrup. "Does that mean one of us is a magnet and the other iron filings?"

She knew which she'd be. "Maybe we're both iron filings being drawn to the giant magnet in the wall."

He arched his neck to look over his shoulder, his skepticism clearly back in place. Laughing, she put her hands flat against his chest and pushed away. She waited for her balance to return, the way it usually did, but if anything, she was even loopier. Her hands wouldn't leave his shirt. Her breath was shallow and shaky. Because she knew he was going to kiss her.

Kiss. His mouth touching her mouth. No. She didn't kiss. Or touch. Or... But no words of protest made it out before his lips touched hers.

Shane kept his hands where they were, even though his first inclination was to touch her face, bury his fingers in her hair and deepen the kiss. But he went for soft. Gentle. Unthreatening. Up till this minute, she'd seemed so skittish, so anxious to avoid contact.

He inhaled deeply, trying to memorize her smell. Fresh

air, hint of pine, some light perfume that might have had a touch of the exotic. Jasmine?

Her skin was as smooth and silky as he'd guessed. Up close, he could see flecks of amber in her pretty eyes. But the moment she registered that he was looking at her while she was looking at him, the spell was broken. She jumped back and in three wobbly steps was out the door.

Being Jenna, she didn't just abandon him, though. No, her sense of responsibility was too great. She braced herself in the doorway as if poised to come to his rescue should he need help.

"Are you okay?" she asked.

No. He definitely was not okay and he had to stop kidding himself that he was. His feelings for her had changed—morphed into a grown-up version of the crush he'd felt in college. Bigger. Stronger. Undeniable. Bordering, God help him, on love.

The idea made his hands shake, and there was a good chance his legs were going to give out.

"Keep one hand on the wall and step this way," she coaxed, her tone worried.

He did as she suggested. Not because he was dizzy. That sensation had passed. But because his knees felt as though the cartilage was made of foam. "I missed lunch. Nobody said anything about hazard pay."

"Let's go back to the office. Mom bought a big selection of candy bars for the snack bar."

Once they were safely outside, she locked the building and started off, but Shane glanced at the other exhibits. He pointed to the one that looked like a WWII Quonset hut. "Wait. What's in that one?"

"Alice's House? Basically, it's just a cement T that's

about five feet by seven feet. Dad built the structure around it to protect visitors when it rains. And it gets pretty windy through here, too."

"Let me guess. It has something to do with Alice in Wonderland?"

"Very good. The tour guide stands the shortest person in the crowd at one end of the T and the tallest person at the other. To the observers in the viewing area, the two appear to be the same height—even if they switch places."

"It's an optical illusion."

"Maybe."

He shook his head. "And over there?" He pointed to the third structure, which had a ramp leading to a door on one end and another ramp on the opposite.

"Well, I know it doesn't look like it from this angle, but between the two buildings is a maze."

"That fence thing?"

She nodded. "It's made of reinforced concrete and the way it's painted makes it almost invisible—unless you're up close."

"Does the U.S. Army know about this?"

She grinned. "Dad's best friend used to be a retired brigadier general with the National Guard. I can't say for sure, but maybe Dad and Stan exchanged state secrets. I kinda doubt it, though."

"Amazing."

She snapped her fingers to get his attention. "For a couple of years, Dad had a terrible problem with graffiti. Then a rumor got around that the maze had mysterious powers and anyone who defaced the walls would suffer impotence and/or infertility." She looked down pointedly. "That's not a can of spray paint in your pocket, is it?"

Shane rarely blushed, but at the moment he was darn glad Coop wasn't there. "That sounds like something one of our characters would say. But which one?"

"My mom's?"

They looked at each other and nodded—some of their earlier camaraderie back. "Her way of getting through the scientist's thick skull that she has the hots for him."

"Yeah. In a way, my dad was like that, too. When he was focused on some problem, he blanked out everything else. Everybody else."

He thought he detected a note of hurt in her tone, but she was out of range before he could ask. Avoidance, he decided, was a mode of self-protection. He could appreciate that. After all, he hadn't been back to Minnesota since his mother died. Not even to attend his father's funeral. When Shane told Adam on the phone he wasn't coming, Adam had hung up on him and they hadn't spoken since.

Avoidance. He was a master of it.

CHAPTER NINE

JENNA CHECKED HER WATCH. She'd given herself plenty of time to get to the wedding, which was at two. But since today was also the grand reopening of the Mystery Spot, she'd felt compelled to put in an appearance to make sure her team had everything under control.

"You look pretty," Robyn Craine, Jenna's new assistant manager, said. They were standing inside the gate watching a family of five join another group waiting to start the tour. The guide was a young man from Detroit who was spending the summer with his grandparents. "I love your dress," Robyn said, tilting her head to give Jenna the once-over. "But, um, please tell me you're wearing different shoes to the ceremony."

The girl, who was barely nineteen, reminded Jenna of herself so many years ago. Obviously, she wasn't afraid to think for herself and voice an opinion.

"Shoes are optional," she said, consulting her checklist one last time. She'd been here since six, and had changed clothes a few minutes earlier in the office to save time. She didn't want to be late for her best friend's wedding, but walking away from her second opening day of the season was killing her. "I meant to get a pedicure but ran out of time."

"Well, I'd still suggest losing the tennis shoes. They make you look like Julia Roberts in *Runaway Bride*."

Jenna glanced up. "You do know I'm not the one getting hitched, right?"

"Everyone knows Libby is marrying the blond hunk from *Are You Ready for Your Close-up?* I saw him in town the other day and nearly peed my pants. He's taller and cuter than he looks on TV. Lucky Libby."

Jenna agreed but not for those reasons. Libby and Cooper were so obviously in love it almost hurt to see them together. Not that she'd spent much time with her friend the past few days. Between getting her crew prepared to re-open and working with Shane every morning, Jenna barely had time to brush her teeth and drop into bed.

But she wasn't complaining. The creative challenge was so exciting and frustrating and demanding she'd never felt more alive. Of course, some of that might have been due to Shane, who pushed but also praised. He was good for her self-esteem, she decided. A girl could get used to someone telling her how smart and clever and creative she was. And she liked spending time with him.

Too much, maybe, given the fact that he was only here for a few more days.

"So, are we good to go here?" she asked, handing Robyn the clipboard.

"You bet. A little slow, but I think things will pick up this afternoon. I'm really excited about your idea of using Jason to stand out near the highway flipping that big arrow around. That was really smart, Jenna."

"Actually, it wasn't my idea, but I'll pass along your kudos to the person who thought of it…if it works. I'll call after the reception to see how our traffic is doing."

Shane's off-the-cuff suggestion had been one of those aha moments. "Why didn't I think of that?" she'd exclaimed, intrigued by the image of a handsome young man in a bright purple T-shirt tossing around a huge yellow arrow.

That's when he'd pointed out that sometimes a person on the outside could see things more clearly than the person who grew up doing something out of habit. That shift in thinking made her start to question other things she'd taken for granted.

She'd always been told that her predilection toward fiction, falling in love with imaginary characters and getting lost in their story, was a liability because it interfered with her ability to think critically and study the kinds of subjects that were deep and important. Like science.

But what if her dad was wrong?

"Call if you want, but you don't have to worry about a thing. We're going to have a great day. I just know it. Have fun." Robyn started toward the office. "Catch the bouquet for me." She paused. "No. On second thought, I don't want it. I have six more years of college. I don't have time for a husband."

Her laugh made Jenna smile. She'd felt the same way when she set off for South Dakota State University. Big dreams. Lots of plans. Until one stupid decision blew everything to pieces.

She shook her head to get rid of the thought and hurried through the gate to her car, which was parked in the front row. The lot was less than a third full and most cars were parked a polite distance apart, even without formal lines on the gravel. Which is probably why she stopped and stared at the car beside hers. It was so close she was going to have to squeeze sideways to open the driver's-side door.

She hoped the driver wasn't one of her employees, who had been told to park on the far side of the lot. She couldn't imagine any of them starting the first day of work by breaking the rules.

She was tempted to go back inside and find the culprit but decided she didn't have time. She kept walking. As she got closer, she realized someone was inside the car. A man. He opened the door and got out as she approached.

A skittering sensation—like the ghostly draft she sometimes felt in Alice's House—shot up her back. She hugged her arms to her chest to keep from shivering. There was gooseflesh on her bare skin. Strange, she thought, given the eighty-degree temperature.

"You just missed a tour, but there'll be another one starting in ten minutes," she said, slowing her pace. She felt an odd reluctance to get too close to him.

"Yes. I was looking over the pamphlet I picked up at my hotel," the man said. His voice held a familiar Midwestern lilt, but he wasn't a local.

Or a tourist, her mind said. Despite the Hawaiian print shirt, which he wore outside of his tan, cotton trousers.

Something about him wasn't quite right, and her heart rate refused to go back to normal. She uncurled her fingertips, which still tingled from the initial adrenaline rush.

"There's a waiting area that has information about the Mystery Spot's history and a diorama of the grounds," she said, pointing him in the direction of the ticket booth. Could the person working the booth see them? she wondered.

He made a noncommittal grunt but didn't move. She

should have found that nonthreatening, but she couldn't shake her uneasiness. Something about him seemed familiar, and she racked her brain to place him. Then it hit her. He was the man from the limo who she'd seen outside the hotel.

She glanced at his car. A Lexus, but probably a rental since it had South Dakota plates. For some reason she didn't find the fancy car reassuring, either.

She knew she was acting peculiarly but she couldn't bring herself to walk to her car until the man was farther away. Something he didn't seem inclined to do. In fact, he leaned his hip on the fender of his car and removed his sunglasses.

Jenna's involuntary intake of air made him look her way. The beard was different. The lines around his eyes more pronounced. He had more gray. But the resemblance was there, if you were looking. This man was Shane's brother. His twin.

He seemed to read her reaction because he said, "I was told I might find my brother here."

Jenna's pulse sped up and she stepped back involuntarily. The heel of her running shoe landed awkwardly on a rock and she stumbled slightly but kept her balance. She didn't understand this irrational fear—that's surely what it was—but she'd learned the hard way to pay attention to her subconscious. "No. He's in town. At a friend's wedding. I'm headed there myself. If you give me your number, I could have him call you."

He didn't look pleased. And the intensity of the look in his eyes was almost enough to send her sprinting back to the Mystery Spot. She stood her ground.

"You don't remember me, do you? Adam Ostergren. We met once. Back in college. I was visit—"

She remembered. "I have to go. Like I said, if you want me to give Shane a message…"

Suddenly the musical jangle of a cell phone sounded. Jenna was surprised, since reception in this part of the mountains was so sketchy. Maybe he was one of the lucky few with satellite connections.

He walked to the door he'd left open and leaned over to locate his phone. The brief distraction was all Jenna needed to dash to her car, shimmy sideways and get in since it wasn't locked. She used the master switch to lock all four doors then started the engine. She didn't look back until he was a small image in her rearview mirror.

Her hands were shaking on the steering wheel and she felt almost giddy with relief but at the same time she felt silly. "Can you say *paranoid?*" she muttered, her face on fire. She wondered if that made her as messed up as her mother, only in a different way.

But no amount of embarrassment was enough to make her turn around and apologize for acting like a crazy woman. She didn't owe Shane's brother anything. If anything, he owed her. He was the last person she remembered talking to that night before everything went haywire. Not that he was ever a suspect. Shane had vouched for Adam's whereabouts at the time of the rape, but Adam had left her in a vulnerable position that someone else took advantage of. That made him scum, in her book.

She wiped an errant tear from the corner of her eye and focused on pushing all the negative thoughts of her past out of her mind. Her best friend in the world was getting married to a great guy who loved her. Whatever Adam wanted was Shane's problem, not hers.

SHANE FELT LIKE A FRAUD. His best friend was getting married and all Shane could think about was Jenna. She'd blown into the gathering as if a ghost were chasing her, then disappeared into the quaint little Hobbit house where the women were doing bridal things. She spared barely a glance in his direction.

Shane had attended a dozen or more weddings over the years, but this one was the most laid-back he'd ever seen. Only the groom seemed uptight.

"Relax, Coop. You're as jumpy as ants in a frying pan." The two men were standing together near a lattice gazebo that looked about a hundred years old with flowering vines and ornamental strawberries encircling the base.

Coop stopped fidgeting long enough to look at Shane. "Ants in a frying pan? Who says things like that?"

"Our character who runs the Oh-Zone. Jenna and I made him from the South. He's an odd-duck loner who moved to this part of the country thirty years ago and set up shop. Started with a roadside attraction that grew and expanded. He's brilliant but self-educated. Just the opposite of her father. Get it?"

Coop nodded. "When do I get to read the first script?"

"I e-mailed a rough draft to my secretary yesterday. She might have something ready for me to print later today."

"Cool. I won't be here, you know."

They'd come as close to a fight over that fact as either could remember in their relationship. Cooper had insisted on taking his bride on a honeymoon. Shane could appreciate the tradition behind the gesture, but given their time constraints, he didn't think two weeks in Bermuda was appropriate. They'd compromised. Libby and Coop were driving to Yellowstone.

"She went there as a child and has never been back," Coop had said. "And we'll only be gone four days. I promise."

Four days. Shane hoped. Not that Coop had been a lot of help, but Shane knew actors. Cooper would have plenty to say about what he saw on the page if it didn't live up to his expectations.

"How late do you expect the reception to run?"

"Six-ish." He made a give-or-take gesture. "Calvin says guests can stay as late as they want. He and Mary will go to bed when they're ready. The caterers will take everything with them when they go, so…I guess it depends on how long Libby wants to stay."

Their conversation ended when a petite fairy in green silk dashed up to them. Char, Shane noticed, had dyed the highlights in her hair pale green to match the ribbons that fell from the waistband of her gathered tulle skirt.

"Give the violinist her cue, Coop. Libby's chomping at the bit—" She made a face. "Forget that. Bad metaphor. She's as serene and together as a regal princess and she's ready to wed her prince. Or, in this case, you."

"Char, why do you always give me such a rough time?"

"Somebody has to do it. Handsome men are all alike. They think they're entitled. I'm just keepin' it real."

Coop looked hurt but only for a fraction of a second, then he gave a little hop. "Okay, then…let's do this."

Char and Kat slipped into their seats in front of the gazebo moments before the music started to play. As scripted, Jenna approached from the side door of the house rather than walk up the middle of the garden where the bride would make her entrance.

Once Jenna was standing at the gazebo directly across from Shane, the rest of the action fell into a gauzy background for him. He tried to pay attention, but his gaze kept returning to her.

Her dress fit as if it had been sewn for her. The fabric was polished cotton, a white background with splashes of color that could have come fresh from an artist's palette. A swirl of cobalt blue lovingly cupped her right breast, which swelled above the scalloped neckline.

"Beautiful," he mouthed.

Her cheeks turned the rosy hue he liked so much.

She wouldn't meet his gaze after that. Instead she turned so she could watch Libby's niece—a tiny vision in pink and white swinging a basket of rose petals as she led the procession. Next came Libby, barefoot and spectacular, on the arm of her brother. The female minister, who had been sitting—praying, Shane assumed—inside the gazebo stepped into place between him and Jenna.

Libby paused near the front of the small audience to slip a white rose from her bouquet and hand it to her grandmother, who was sitting in a wheelchair beside Calvin. She pressed a kiss on the elderly woman's cheek then whispered, "I love you, Gran. Thank you, Cal."

The intimate nature of the garden setting made it possible for everyone to hear her. Shane saw Jenna's mother wipe a tear from her eyes.

Her grandmother smiled benignly, while calming the excited toy pooch on her lap.

"Dear friends and family of Elizabeth and Cooper, please join us in a prayer of love and good wishes for this couple."

Shane didn't pay too much attention to the actual vows.

He was too busy staring at Jenna. Something wasn't right. Her smile seemed frozen in place. She wasn't the same person he talked to on the phone a few hours earlier. He'd called to let her know his secretary was cleaning up the notes they'd sent her and they should have a legitimate script for revisions later today. She'd been upbeat and positive. He'd detected no trace of fear or worry in her voice, but that's exactly what he saw in her eyes.

When prodded by Cooper, Shane managed to produce the plain gold band Libby had insisted on. Moments later he bowed his head and joined the minister in praying for the married couple's happiness. He applauded on cue and shook Coop's hand and kissed the bride's cheek. But the moment he had his chance, he stepped beside Jenna and whispered, "What's wrong? Something happened."

"Later."

The slight tremor in her voice told him whatever the problem it was serious. They joined the short procession, but when they reached the end of the row of a raised bed filled with frothy green carrot tops, he took her hand and pulled her toward a weeping willow at the far edge of the garden. The lush drapery of green leaves provided an illusion of privacy. He kept a prudent distance between them in case people were looking. "Tell me."

She looked toward the reception area. "It's no biggie. I just feel stupid. Your brother showed up at the Mystery Spot and for some reason I overreacted."

Adam is here? He tried to loosen the top button of his shirt, but his fingers wouldn't cooperate.

"What did he say?"

"Just that he was told he could find you there." She hugged herself as if cold, but he knew that wasn't the case.

"When you see him, maybe you could apologize for me. I'm not good with strangers, especially strange men. And even after I recognized him...well...I told him I'd give you the message that he was in town, then I jumped into my car and drove away." She looked at him. "I wasn't exactly polite. In fact, I sorta panicked. I haven't done that in years."

He should have known his brother would show up eventually. Playing ostrich never worked in the past where Adam was concerned.

He let out a low, furious string of cuss words.

Her eyes went wide. "You weren't kidding. You two really don't get along, do you?"

"I haven't seen him in years. The last time we spoke on the phone was after my father died. When I told him I wasn't going to the funeral and didn't give a damn what he did with the estate."

"Why? What happened between you?"

What happened to her happened between them, but he couldn't tell her that. Or could he? Maybe with both his mother and father dead, Shane could rethink the validity of his vow. He didn't owe his brother an ounce of loyalty. But would reopening the case be in Jenna's best interest? His mother's deathbed confession would be considered hearsay. Was that enough to bring charges against Adam? Maybe he should talk to a lawyer before he involved Jenna—for her sake, not his brother's.

"Look," he said, stalling. "I'm sorry he scared you. Adam can be damn intimidating when he wants to be. But now's not the time or place to get into this. As maid of honor and best man, we both have toasts to make, right?"

She frowned but finally nodded.

He took her hand—more gently this time—and parted the curtain of green to lead them back to the festivities. Glasses of champagne were being served by waiters in black pants and white shirts. As they neared the others, she tried to pull her fingers free but he wasn't ready to let go. Once she found out the truth, she'd never let him touch her again. He knew that for certain.

CHAPTER TEN

JENNA EASED BACK in the garden swing and drained her third glass of champagne. She wasn't usually much of a drinker—and three glasses of bubbly over four hours wasn't that extravagant—but if she closed her eyes she felt a little light-headed. That could be a reaction to Shane's presence, she acknowledged.

He'd barely left her side all afternoon. Even now, she saw him checking on her from time to time as he helped load suitcases into the back of the small, sporty Subaru Tribeca SUV that Cooper had given Libby as a wedding present.

"It has third-row seating for all those kids we're going to have," Coop had said, causing Libby to roll her eyes and shake her head.

Libby and Jenna had said their goodbyes earlier. In private. Jenna truly couldn't be happier for her friend. She'd never seen Libby more optimistic about the future and at peace with the past. Was it wrong to feel so wistful? Jenna wondered.

She wasn't sure she'd ever be free from the haunting memory of that night. Until the dream returned she'd begun to believe that she'd turned the page on that chapter of her life. Then, this morning, Shane's brother appeared.

A stranger, and even though she'd been in broad daylight in a public place, she'd felt a panic attack.

She'd suffered them frequently when she first moved home. The humiliating, unpreventable response when fear flooded her body had embarrassed her beyond words and was the main reason she hadn't been able to return to school.

Writing poetry had helped. And time. But obviously she was still not cured.

Beep. Beep.

She looked up as the pretty white car started to inch past the few remaining guests. She sat forward and waved but made no effort to join the others. Libby would understand.

"It went well, wouldn't you say?"

Her heart rate spiked but only for a second or two as her brain recognized Shane as a friend, not a foe. "Y-yes," she answered, her voice a bit tentative. She cleared her throat and added, "It was beautiful. Very Libby."

Shane laughed as he stepped near. "So not Cooper. At least, not the Cooper I used to know. I think it's safe to say Libby has changed him. For the better. He's less frenetic and more focused. Sort of grown up."

Neither said anything for a moment, then Shane asked, "May I join you?"

So polite. He had nice manners. "Sure," she said, scooting over a little.

His weight made the chair creak slightly. The unit was the type that had a built-in canopy with braided fringe around the top. They rocked together finding a complementary rhythm.

Would sex with him be like that, too? Like they'd known each other forever?

She inhaled sharply, shocked by the question that had left her tingling all over. *What's wrong with me?*

"What?" he asked.

She grabbed the first thought that came to mind. "Did I tell you Mom's delirious about her trip to L.A.? You are serious about this screen test, aren't you? She really does have a chance at the Aggie part? You're not just stringing her along to get on my good side?"

His left eyebrow shot upward with a look of incredulity. "Why would I do that? I like Bess. I think she may be very talented. Aggie the dog lady will make a strong secondary character. But I can't hire her without seeing her on screen. It doesn't work that way."

"Oh." She knew that. He'd explained it to her before, but she still couldn't quite believe that her mother might actually appear on a network television show someday. "I feel like a mother sending her kid off to kindergarten. What if nobody likes her? She'll be heartbroken. And I'll have to handle whatever new diseases she contracts after she gets home."

He let his head drop back to rest against the seat. "I wish I could guarantee her a job, but ultimately it's up to her. And the studio. And the test audiences. The entire series has a lot of hurdles to clear before we get a slot in the new lineup."

"I know. I was joking about the new diseases. Did I tell you she's gone off every over-the-counter medicine she was taking before you came and says she feels great? Thank you for that, Shane. No matter what happens."

"No matter what happens," he repeated. His tone was dark and faintly ominous. She knew the subject had changed and they were no longer talking about her mother and the future of the show.

She turned to look at him. "Have you heard from your brother, yet?"

"No. He won't call. I'm sure he's counting on you to give me the message."

"What message? I didn't stick around long enough for him to tell me anything."

When his gaze met hers, she felt a sudden chill.

"You don't look anything alike, by the way," she said, suddenly feeling nervous. "He looks ten years older than you. Dissipated, but very prosperous. I realized that I'd seen him get out of a limo when I was in town wedding-dress shopping."

"Did he see you?"

She shook her head, again unnerved by the intense quality she heard in his voice. There was no love lost between these two, she realized. "Why do you think he's here?"

"Whatever it is, it's not because he missed me. Adam doesn't do warm and fuzzy. Never has."

Jenna didn't think of Shane as a cuddly teddy bear, either, but she was beginning to see him as a Bernese mountain dog. His brother had rottweiler written all over him. And not the sweet kind.

"How can twins be so different?" she asked, without meaning to say the words out loud.

"I've asked myself that a thousand times over the years."

He sounded so hurt and morose, she had no choice but to lean closer and brush aside a lock of his hair. "I like your hair a lot better. And his beard reminds me of the old G.I. Joe dolls—only with gray in it." Her fingers trailed lightly down the side of his jaw. She was glad he was clean shaven.

He covered her hand with his. "We should talk."

"Can we just make out, instead?" she asked, wondering if it was the wedding or the champagne that made her take risks she wasn't in the habit of taking.

"You don't make this easy," he said softly, pulling her into his arms.

His kiss was unlike any they'd shared before. Rough, intense, needy. As if they were the last people on the planet and the world was about to implode. She gave him what she thought he wanted in return, and the heat between them turned molten.

A part of her brain was conscious of where they were, and although it was getting late and the guests had scattered, she wasn't in the habit of making out in public. She pulled back enough to say, "We should go somewhere else. Your place, I'm thinking."

"My place?"

"Coop's gone. My mother is at my house." She looked at him, wondering what was going through his mind.

His eyes seemed shuttered, and he let out a sigh, but instead of making some kind of excuse, which is what she expected, he took her hand and stood, pulling her with him. "I have somewhere better in mind, but we can't get there barefoot. Tell me you have shoes in your car."

She knew intuitively where he wanted to take her—Pactola. Her writing place.

She gave him a quick squeeze. "Tennis shoes and…a flashlight. I could be a Boy Scout, I'm so well prepared."

He laughed and kissed her again. "You have no idea how glad I am that you're not a Boy Scout."

It took them about twenty minutes to actually leave the premises. Caterer questions. A lost dog. Two friends who seemed curious and concerned about Jenna's obvious attachment to Coop's best man.

But finally they were in his car and driving along the highway. Their designated parking spot was empty, which he took as a good sign. And by the time they started along the trail, the moon was high enough in the sky that they barely needed the flashlight Jenna was carrying.

"When my brother and I were kids, we used to sneak out of our parents' cabin at Green Lake and play commando," he said, surprised by a memory that didn't hold some unpleasant overtones.

She was holding his hand. The blanket he'd handed her was clutched to her chest with her free hand. "Normally, I'm more of a daytime girl."

He didn't have to ask to know why. Guilt made him walk a little faster.

She squeezed his hand. "Are we on a schedule?"

He stopped and kissed her. His last, he figured. He made it a good one.

"Wow," she said on a shaky breath, "I just—wow."

He wasn't sure exactly when he realized that he loved her. Maybe he'd always loved her and all that fantasizing and pedestal-propping he'd done with her memory had been a clever way to keep his heart from breaking.

And now he was going to lose her. *Figures*. Adam had cost him so much over the years—pride, self-esteem, their father's affection and respect. How fitting that he would ruin this for Shane, too.

With renewed resignation he started walking again.

"So," she said, "I gather your problems with your brother started later on. When you were kids, the two of you had fun together, huh?"

Fun? Maybe. Some of the time. But every so often their great adventure would turn dark and dangerous. "Adam's always been moody and volatile. If he was in a good mood, life was calm and fairly pleasant. If something didn't go his way or he felt ignored, he'd act out, for want of a better term. Usually I'd get dragged along because he made it impossible to say no. He'd hound, belittle, bribe and cajole—anything to get his way."

When she didn't say anything, he added, "One time he wanted to go window peeking on this high school girl whose family was renting a cabin a few houses down from ours. He looked down on renters, and he called her a slut even though she never gave us the time of day. When I refused to go, he climbed up on my bed—I had the top bunk—and kneeled at the foot of the mattress and started to pee beside where I lying. He said he'd tell Father that I wet the bed."

She made a sound of disgust. "How old were you?"

"Nine or ten. Old enough to talk dirty even though we didn't know the first thing about anything."

They'd reached her writing place. When the idea to come here first popped into his head, he'd seen it as the perfect place to tell her about Adam, but now that they'd arrived here, it struck him what a bad idea that really was. Would the peace and safety she felt here be compromised by the memories he was about to dredge up?

Regretfully, he decided it was too late to turn back. He let go of her hand to spread the blanket while she held the flashlight. The air temperature had to be in the eighties. Not muggy hot, but there were still mosquitoes around. They'd doused each other in bug spray before leaving the parking area.

He killed the light and invited her to sit.

"Thanks for being such a good sport about this," he said.

She sat back on her elbows and looked skyward. "It's okay. In fact, it's perfect. Mrs. Smith's isn't exactly romantic. And you sure couldn't see as many stars. There's Cassiopeia. The Queen's Chair. She was the mother of Andromeda, but because of her vanity she has to spend part of the year upside down."

"I didn't know that. But, if we were back home and it was winter, I'd show you my telescope. When the sky's clear enough, you can see the Orion nebula."

She cocked her head. "Is the sky ever clear? I heard you have terrible air pollution from all the cars on your highways."

"Good point."

"How do you handle it?"

"Same way you handle winter. You complain a little and live through it."

Her laugh made him happy. "Good point."

They sat in companionable silence a few minutes longer, then Jenna turned to him and said, "We're not here to make mad passionate love, are we?"

The moment of truth. The black moment in the story when all hope for a love match comes crashing down, burying the hero under a thick pile of rubble of his own making.

"I don't think you're even going to want to get in the same car with me after I tell you what I need to tell you."

She sat up. "The show's been canceled before it even got made."

He shook his head. "That could still happen, but as of

this moment we're still on track. What I have to tell you has nothing to do with the show. It has to do with you. With what happened to you in college."

Even in the silvery shadows cast by the moonlight through the trees, he could read her reaction. "I don't want to talk about that."

"I'm not surprised, but there's something—"

She put her hand on his arm. "No, Shane. I mean it. If you finished reading my book of poems you'd see that I went through all the stages of grief. I was angry and in denial. I pleaded with every higher power on record to make it all a bad dream. I blamed everyone, but mostly myself. Finally, I forgave everyone, including myself."

His heart thudded heavily in his chest. "Including the man who raped you?"

She jerked her hand back. "Why are you doing this?"

He leaned forward, hands fisted in his lap. "I came to South Dakota with Cooper knowing there was a good chance we'd meet. I couldn't be sure you still lived in Sentinel Pass, but I never forgot the name of the place. Remember in class when the instructor made us stand up and tell something picturesque about our hometown? You made Sentinel Pass sound like a place I knew in my heart, without ever visiting."

"Seriously? I remember being so nervous I swallowed my gum. I have no idea what I said."

"You talked about catching butterflies with your best friend in a green meadow filled with waving grass that tickled your legs."

She made a quiet sound. "Libby and me."

"And there were other times, too, that I overheard you talking with your friends. That probably makes me sound like a stalker, but it wasn't like that. You just talked with such passion and joy that I couldn't help but listen, too."

"And that's why you came here? To find me?"

"When Coop read me Libby's e-mail, the name clicked and I knew I had to come to see for myself if you were still here. If you were okay. Happy. Living the life you'd talked about in college."

"But you barely knew me in college. We couldn't have exchanged more than a dozen words. I was too shy and you were too cool."

His laugh sounded caustic to his ears. "I hid behind that beard and long hair you thought was so hip. It was my pathetic attempt to distance myself from my family—in particular, my clean-cut, ROTC-type brother."

"Why?"

"I don't know the exact moment, but at some point, I realized that Adam wasn't just temperamental or high-strung or moody. He was amoral, narcissistic and lacked any sense of boundaries. Our father called him a chip off the old block. Our mother pretended nothing was wrong."

"So you split."

"Sooner rather than later. In high school I was the one in trouble. I smoked pot, let my hair grow, ran with a crowd my father didn't approve of. Adam was a National Honors Scholar, played in the band and was senior class president." He looked at her. "You're the kind of girl he would have dated. Never for very long. Girls talked. Pretty soon he had a reputation for liking rough sex. But he was very charismatic. I saw him talk girls into things they had no intention of doing. It was all about power."

He could tell by her rapt look that he had her complete attention. She was quick enough to know where this was going and draw her own conclusion, but it was too late to take the easy way out.

"I'd told my mother I was thinking of changing my major to film. My father was mortified. He even called me to say what an embarrassment it would be to him if I 'went off the deep end,' as he put it."

Why can't you, for once, be more like your brother?

"Why would that be embarrassing?"

"My father came from money. Bankers, lawyers, politicians. Anything in the arts was too bohemian for his taste. My grandfather called Joseph McCarthy his friend. What does that tell you?"

"Got it."

"So, Adam made a surprise visit to Brookings to see me. He was attending Loyola. There was talk of him doing an internship with some congressman the following summer. He was very smug and full of himself, and he promised Dad that by the end of the weekend he'd have talked some sense into me."

She didn't say anything, but he could read her growing tension in her body language. "I knew how to play the game, Jenna. All I had to do was nod and pretend to agree, then do my own thing once the furor had passed. That's what I always did growing up. It's how my mother managed to stay married to my father for forty-some years.

"But, for some reason, that weekend I snapped. I just couldn't take being bullied by my own twin anymore. We had a huge fight. I stormed out and went to the party. Adam followed."

Jenna frowned. "I remember seeing you come in. You walked past me as if I wasn't there and grabbed a bottle of beer like you'd just crossed the Sahara."

He nodded. "My goal was to get smashed. I scored some weed and was hanging out in the garage with the other stoners when somebody told me Adam was there. I looked in through the window and saw him talking to you. You were laughing. That's when I left."

"Where'd you go?" she asked, her voice squeaking a tiny bit.

"I hit a couple of bars. I was passed out when Adam came in. I woke up because he was packing to leave and making so damn much noise. I looked at the clock and it said three-eiteen. He told me he'd been watching TV but he couldn't sleep and was heading home. I took him at his word."

She edged back slightly. "I have a feeling I know where you're going with this, but if you're going to accuse your brother of being the guy who raped me, now—fifteen or whatever years later—you have to remember that you provided him with an alibi."

"I honestly couldn't see him doing anything to jeopardize his prescribed future. He never had any trouble getting girls to go to bed with him. There was no reason whatsoever to think he would have attacked you."

"*Drugged* and attacked," she corrected, in a tight voice. "But now you think differently, right?"

He was about to break his promise to his mother, but first he had to make her understand that she wasn't the only one whose life had been impacted by this act. "What happened to you changed me, Jenna. I can't explain it completely, but seeing you in the backseat of your parents' car…all the hope and possibilities I'd read in your face every time we passed on campus gone. I dropped out of school without telling anybody. I let my mother know that

I was alive and living in Los Angeles, but I didn't see any member of my family again until my mother's hospice provider called to tell me she was dying."

"Oh, Shane, that must have killed you."

Her hand on his arm was warm and comforting. Too bad it wouldn't last. "I caught the first flight to Minneapolis and rented a car. She was being cared for in our family home. Neither my brother nor my father was there. Just some strangers who made sure she had the proper dose of morphine."

"I'm so sorry."

"She was only lucid for short intervals, but it was as if she'd bottled up all these *things* she needed to get off her chest before she died. She told me she'd always known about my father's mistresses. Dozens over the years. She'd stopped keeping track…or caring. She'd done the best she could to be happy, knowing full well that she'd traded security, a nice house and a prominent place in society for a life of her own."

Jenna sighed. "My mother gave up her dreams to live my father's. I think this was pretty common of women in their generation."

Her kindness made what he was about to say all the more difficult. "I remember feeling so sorry for her, and she kept saying that I was her crowning glory. The one who got away before becoming totally corrupted by the darkness. She blamed my father's side of the family. Like it was a blood curse or something. I thought her bitterness or the cancer had poisoned her mind, but then she mumbled something about birthing a rapist."

Jenna's hand fell away. "How could she…why would she think—?"

"He told her. Adam went home when he left Brookings. Apparently, he'd panicked. Dad was gone, so Mom heard his confession, so to speak."

The night had gone still, even the crickets were silent. "She told you this?"

"The next time she was lucid, I asked her directly. She wept. She said she'd spent every moment since wondering if he would do it again. Ruin another woman's life. Get arrested and wind up in jail. I thought she was going to die right that minute she was so upset. I called for the nurse, but as we waited for the woman to come, my mother begged me to keep my brother's secret. She swore he never did anything like that again. He'd been curious about the drug he'd heard about. He told her the girl never said no."

Jenna jumped to her feet. "I would have. If I'd had the chance. He took that ability away from me. I never would have chosen to do what he did to me. He was horrible. Brutal. I needed stitches, for God's sake. He damaged me not just physically but emotionally, at a core level, and then he justified this because I didn't say no?"

His mother had cried in her weak raspy voice, "He's not a rapist, Shane. He's not. It was a mistake. He was caught up in the moment. He promised me it would never happen again. And it never did. I'm certain of it. I've watched him carefully. It's one of the reasons I stayed with your father, so I could keep an eye on Adam. You have to believe me, son, and you have to promise not to tell another soul. Swear to it, Shane. Give me your word."

He'd had no choice but to ease her guilt and let her pass in peace.

"He and I have never spoken of this. I assumed he didn't

know I knew, although I left a few hours after Mom's funeral, so he might have guessed."

"And you think he's here because of that?"

"I don't know, but I can tell you that he has a highly public career that could be destroyed by an accusation of rape, even if such an allegation couldn't be proven. Jenna, I'd planned to call a lawyer this week, but I thought I'd have time before I left. I'm not telling you what to do, but I don't think a secondhand deathbed confession would be enough to reopen the case, let alone prove it."

"Is that why you're here? The real reason?"

"It's one of the reasons. Like I said, I needed to see for myself how you were coping. If you'd moved on and were happy in a life of your choosing."

"Maybe offer me a job as a scriptwriter to ease your conscience? Just how guilty do you feel, Shane? Would you give my mom a role in the show even if she can't act her way out of a wet paper sack? Were you prepared to sleep with me? If I'm over this enough to have sex, then I must be fixed, huh?"

He got to his feet. "Jenna, you have every right to hate me. I can't defend myself or my brother. I've struggled with this guilt for six years. In complete honesty, I might not have ever told you if Adam hadn't shown up. Not for his sake, believe me. For yours. He's rich, connected and powerful. At the very least, he could make your life miserable."

"He already has." She started away.

"Wait. Take the flashlight."

"I can see fine. You need it worse than me. Just hurry. I want to go home."

He grabbed the quilt and the flashlight and followed her.

They didn't speak again until they reached her driveway. "Don't pull in. Mom's probably asleep by now and the windows will be open. I don't want to wake her. Tomorrow's a big day. Her trip to L.A."

"Are you taking her to the airport?"

"Yes."

"If I can get you a seat on the plane, would you consider going with her?"

She looked at him a full minute. "No. Final answer. I'm not running away from anything ever again. I haven't decided what to do about your brother policewise. When I do decide, I'll let you know. In the meantime, I'm done working on the scripts. I have a business to run and that's all I'm focusing on at the moment. I hope you won't let my decision influence Mom's chances where the show is concerned, but I can't work with someone whose values are so screwed up he'd let a rapist walk around free. I'm just glad I didn't see you go anywhere near the champagne this afternoon."

A low blow. Not undeserved, but it hurt all the same. He wasn't the kind of man who'd spike his date's drink. He'd never hurt a woman in his life, but why should he expect her to believe that? Maybe he was guilty by association. He sure as hell felt guilty. And a little sick to his stomach.

She got out and, to his surprise, didn't slam the door. He watched her walk inside, her back straight and proud. He swallowed against the tightness in his throat and put the car in gear. As he drove through the quiet streets of Sentinel Pass, he actually felt close to breaking down. Not only had he lost the girl, he'd lost out on any chance of ever being a part of the town he'd pictured in his mind so clearly over the years. He wondered if Coop had left any sleeping pills behind. He had a feeling this was going to be a long, sleepless night.

it has many of the town's businesses looking for new sponsors. Meanwhile, the station will remain off the air until the clerk had a chat by the Alex couldn't make it, so Jenna might...

CHAPTER ELEVEN

SHANE GOT UP EARLY the next morning, despite his lack of sleep. He'd called every number he once had for his brother and even tried the Alex Johnson Hotel where Jenna had mentioned seeing Adam. The grumpy clerk told him no one by the name of Adam Ostergren was registered.

Shane knew better than to think his brother had simply given up and gone home. That wasn't Adam. His brother was focused, tenacious and unforgiving. As far as Shane knew, Adam had never forgiven him for being born.

He poured a second cup of coffee and was about to try Coop's cell when his phone rang. "Reynard here."

"Reynard. Chosen because you were our mother's favorite?"

He set down his cup and walked into the living room to stand beside the home's large picture window. He'd found the exact spot to ensure a good connection. "Hello, A."

Adam had always hated the diminutive nickname.

"When you didn't bother letting me know you were in the area, I decided I should come check things out for myself. A new television project everyone is talking about. Wouldn't Dad be proud?"

Shane wasn't in the mood for small talk. "What will it take to get you to leave her alone?"

"I don't have any idea what you're talking about."

"Of course you do. That's why you showed up at the Mystery Spot. To send a message to me. She's vulnerable. You're powerful. Got it. Now, what do you need to disappear?"

The pause that followed was so long Shane thought the call might have gotten dropped, but as he was about to repeat the question, his brother said, "I knew I couldn't trust the bitch."

"Jenna?"

"Mom. I sensed that she told you, but I couldn't exactly come right out and ask, could I?"

"Why'd you tell her? You and Mom were never close."

"Not like the two of you. But Dad was gone on one of his fake fact-finding trips boinking his then-current mistress in New Guinea or something. I was afraid the police were going to show up, and I had this stupid scratch on my face. That's why I left while it was still dark. I knew you'd ask questions and eventually figure it out. Mom guessed the truth and she wasn't half as intuitive as you were."

If Adam had sounded even the least bit repentant or had asked about Jenna, Shane might have been inclined to give him the benefit of the doubt. But this was classic Adam mode—ready to blame someone else for his decisions. Growing up, Shane usually had been his scapegoat.

"Well, if it makes you feel any better Mom never mentioned it until she was dying. I think she needed to relieve herself of the burden so she could go in peace. I figured keeping her secret was the least I could do since I'd basically abandoned her to you and Dad all those years."

"Spoken like a true bleeding-heart California liberal.

Mom made her own bed. A very cushy one. If she'd wanted out, all she had to do was ask. Toward the end, Dad would have given her a divorce in a heartbeat so he could be with Christina."

Shane had guessed that the woman his father married a mere eight weeks after burying his first wife had been involved with him longer. That she was closer in age to Shane and Adam hadn't surprised him, either.

"Mom's reasons for staying in such a sick relationship were entirely her own. That's in the past. I want to know what you intend to do where Jenna Murphy is concerned."

"I guess part of that depends on what she intends to do with the information I assume you shared with her. Which, I should add, was a very selfish thing to do."

"Selfish?"

"I know you, Shanely." Shane ground his teeth at the nickname. "Mom's deathbed confession has been eating at you for years. You probably set this whole TV ball in motion just so you come here and lay this heartfelt confession at her feet. Did she thank you for opening that particular festering can of worms?"

Hardly.

"You raped her, Adam. And went on to live your life with impunity. Where's the justice in that?"

Adam's laugh set the hair on the back of Shane's neck on end. "Oh, please. Don't tell me you're so damn naive you actually believe in justice. The only thing that matters in this world is money. Find out how much this is going to cost, and we'll all go back to living our lives."

Shane shook his head. "Reverse blackmail. Interesting concept. I guarantee you money never crossed Jenna's mind."

"Then it will be up to you to make her see the light. This can go away and she comes out with a healthy bank account—or things can get ugly." He paused. "And I do mean ugly. I think you know what I'm talking about. Does the name Linda Scoggins ring any bells?"

The line went dead.

Shane heaved the phone at the sofa with all his might. It bounced and landed on the floor a few feet away. He stared at it a few minutes, his chest heaving as if he'd run a race with the devil. In a way he'd been racing this particular demon his whole life. And now Jenna was caught in the crosshairs.

Linda Scoggins. A girl they'd known in grade school. Pudgy. Glasses. Pigtails. Those were the only images that came to mind, but the horror of her death had left a lasting impression on Shane. She'd slipped through the ice on a pond in their neighborhood. An accident.

Shane had never thought otherwise, but now he remembered something that he hadn't realized he knew. Linda had tattled on Adam a few weeks before her death. She'd told the teacher that Adam had unzipped his pants and wiggled his penis at her in the cloakroom during recess. The Ostergrens had been called to the school for a conference. Shane hadn't been privy to the whole debacle, but he'd overheard some of the fight between his mother and father that followed.

"He needs to see a doctor," his mother had cried. "Our son is sick. If we don't get him help now, I won't be responsible for what happens in the future."

"When have you ever been responsible for any damn thing in your life or anyone else's?" his father had shouted. "Adam is fine. Just a little high-spirited. Stop your squawking and get out of my sight."

Shane's hand was shaking when he bent to pick up his phone. He needed to find Jenna and convince her to take Adam's offer. More than anything, he prayed she hadn't already contacted the police.

He called the Murphy home but there was no answer.

He cursed and picked up his keys. "Why the hell doesn't she have a cell phone?"

JENNA TAPPED THE HORN impatiently as she passed a slow-moving pickup truck towing a gigantic travel trailer. She wasn't in a hurry—they'd allowed plenty of time before her mother's flight—but her lack of sleep had left her tense and grouchy.

"Your father used to get like this before I went any-where. He could make life so miserable the week before a trip, I was always tempted to cancel."

Jenna wasn't upset about her mother's trip, but she let the implication stand. Better than admitting the true cause of her bad mood. "Maybe that explains why we didn't take more family vacations, huh?"

"What are you talking about? We couldn't get away in summer, but we traveled in the off-season. Remember the Thanksgiving we spent in Washington, D.C.?"

"That's right. We ate turkey dinner in the hotel restaurant and they ran out of pumpkin pie."

Bess made a sad sound. "You cried and your dad felt so bad the next day he found a bakery and bought you a whole one."

"He said I didn't need to share."

"But you did, of course. Because that's your nature. You're generous and kind and you think of others."

The praise felt good considering how much soul-searching she'd done in the wee hours. Her mind kept going to the night of the attack, probing deep for details that might have given some warning of what kind of man Adam Ostergren was. Had she done something to lead him on? Provoke him?

Over and over in the months following the rape, she'd asked a nonresponsive God, "Why me?" She still didn't have an answer. In fact, all she had was more questions. Would reopening the case provide the sense of closure she'd always lacked? Would the D.A. be able to get a conviction from Shane's testimony? She'd seen her share of television court dramas and knew that hearsay was usually disallowed as evidence.

"What's wrong, Jenna? You don't think I should do this, do you? Did Shane say something? Am I wasting my time?"

Jenna hadn't brought up Shane's confession because she didn't want her mother to worry or, worse, cancel her trip. Bess had given up her dream often enough in the past because her family needed her. Not this time.

"No, Mom. In fact, Shane said he thinks you have a good chance. It's all up to you."

"Darn. I was afraid of that. What business do I have thinking I'm good enough to be on TV? No fool like an old fool, right?"

"Mom, you're in the prime of your life. You're healthier than you've been in years. I'm sorry I'm so out of it this morning. The wedding… Shane and I… You're the only part of my life that's going right. I smile every time I look at you because you finally look like you're having fun."

"Really?" Her mom took a deep breath. Shaky, but not quite as panicky as her breathing had sounded a minute earlier.

"A few weeks ago you were a walking pharmacy. Now, you're on your way to Los Angeles."

"To take my first ever screen test." The last came out with a girlish squeal.

Jenna grinned. "I'm excited for you, Mom. And I know you're going to be great. You're happy with the way Shane and I wrote your character, right? Aggie Dupree."

"Also known as Aggie the dog lady. I love her. She's a hoot. A great foil for Libby's character since you decided her grandmother had passed away. Aggie's the right balance of whacko and real person. And I love the way she adores Louie, your father's character. I know just how she feels about wanting love in your life again but being wary of all the *stuff* that comes with it."

Jenna glanced sideways. "Do you think you'd like to remarry some day?"

Her mother's cheeks colored slightly. "In all honesty, I'd like what Mary and Calvin have. A private understanding between the two of them, without getting their children in an uproar about inheritances."

The thought had never crossed Jenna's mind, but she could see how the future might turn complex in many ways if her mother found someone new. She wondered if someday they'd look back over the past two years as their transitional period of mourning. Double the traditional length since there were two of them.

She realized she was ready for a change, too. Which was strange since she'd always been the one who advocated the importance of maintaining the status quo.

"We had a good opening day yesterday," she said, taking her usual shortcut through a residential neighborhood. They passed by a handsome independent-living manor. Her parents had joked about winding up there when they were too old to climb the stairs to the second-floor bedroom. She suddenly missed her father so much she had to fight back tears.

Swallowing, she went on. "Robyn did a fabulous job. She's really fired up about taking on as much responsibility as I want to give her. Unusual for a girl her age, don't you think?"

"Not really. You were the same way before you went to college. Your father used to say the word *can't* wasn't part of your vocabulary."

"Really? I don't remember that."

"Ah…well, Clarence was a typical absentminded professor. He'd think something and not remember if he said it aloud. But he loved you very much and was always proud of you."

"Except at the end, you mean."

"Always," Mom stressed. "As a father he was tortured by guilt. He blamed himself for pushing you to go to college—even though intellectually he knew a rape could have happened anywhere. It was his inability to protect you that came across as disapproval."

"He didn't think I was a coward?"

Mom let out a sharp sound of dismay. "Jenna Mae Murphy, how can you say such a thing? You suffered the loss of innocence. Your father knew what that was like. His parents died in a fire while he was in college. He worked three jobs to finish his degree and saw classmates who didn't have his grades get the best jobs because of their connections. He nursed that grudge for a long time. Until he met me, actually. You and your dad were a lot alike, but you have my Molly Brown attitude, too, girlfriend, and don't you forget it."

Jenny chuckled at her stern tone. "O-o-kay."

They traveled in silence for a few miles, Jenna digesting the information about her father. She'd heard the tragic story of her grandparents' deaths but had never really thought about how that might have impacted her father— a young man who suddenly found the course of his life altered forever. He'd needed to help provide for his younger sister, who was in high school at the time. She'd gone to live with relatives in Montana. When Jenna stayed with her after the rape, her aunt had told her that Clarence had continued to send money every month, urging her to go to college so she could be independent and would never have to feel like a burden.

Education. His answer for everything. *No wonder Dad pushed me so hard to go back to school.* And she'd let one miserable excuse for a human being take that from her.

"Mom, how come Shane isn't going with you? Doesn't the director need to be present for screen tests?"

Bess repositioned the printed copy of her electronic ticket in her oversize purse between her Sudoku book and the copy of the script Jenna had given her. "I got the impression he was staying here to finish up the scripts. He said something about slipstreams or video conferences... I don't know. I wasn't really paying attention. There are times when I think I'm in the middle of a dream. What would your father say?"

Jenna stopped at the light. She turned and eyed the woman who looked ten years younger than she had a week ago. If nothing came of this, Jenna would still be grateful to Shane for giving Mom a chance to realize her dream. "Dad would be pouting because you were leaving, but the minute you got on the plane, he'd start telling everyone how wonderful you were going to do. The next Doris Day or something."

"Doris Day? Oh, dear. I hope not. She was a little before my time. How 'bout Meryl Streep?"

"Works for me."

As they neared the turn for the airport, her mother said, "Are you going to tell me what happened last night between you and Shane before I leave, or am I going to have to worry all the way to L.A.?"

"We drove to the lake and talked. I…I don't think we're going to work together anymore."

Bess inhaled sharply. "You can't be serious."

"Mom, it was inevitable. It's not like we have a future together. His life is on the West Coast. He's only here for a few more days at most. Even if you win the part, can you see us moving to California?"

"Yes."

"Really?"

Her mom waited until Jenna pulled into a parking place before saying, "Jenna Mae, please tell me you're not going to do this again."

"Do what?"

"Let your past muck up your future. I've seen the sparks between you two. And one thing I know about a Bernese mountain dog, they bond for life."

Jenna couldn't help but chuckle, despite the intensity of her mother's tone. "Shane is a great guy, Mom. And he'd make a wonderful dog, but I'm not ready to be a pet owner."

Bess closed her eyes and sighed. "Honey, you know I'm talking metaphorically. He's genuine, deep and real. Give him a chance to prove it."

Tears filled her eyes. "I tried, Mom. But…it's complicated."

Bess hugged her. "Life is, honey. Start to finish. Just don't let your fears keep you from playing." She smiled. "I'd better go before I start channeling my character. Aggie would tell you that the right dog can mean the difference between a night of peaceful sleep with a warm body beside you and a cold bleak future. You're a smart girl. You'll figure it out."

She opened the door. "Don't bother coming in. I only have my carry-on bag. See you in a couple of days."

Jenna got out anyway and rushed around the front of the car to hug her mother fiercely. "Knock 'em dead, Mom. You're going to be great."

Bess hugged her back, then snapped the handle of her small wheeled bag into the tote position and started toward the building. Jenna couldn't bear to watch her walk away. Her heart was too bruised. She was going to have to decide what to do about Adam, soon. And her mother was right. She couldn't let fear shape her decision. That meant she needed to talk to Shane.

She got in the car but couldn't bring herself to turn the key in the ignition.

Shane.

Against her will, she closed her eyes and brought his image to mind. That roguish look in his eyes whenever she said something that amused him. How could one nonsmile make her feel so smart and clever? And in the moonlight last night the pain she'd read in his eyes had broken her heart…after her initial flush of anger had passed. He'd been a victim, too, he'd said. Yet he'd been brave enough to face her.

She rested her head on the steering wheel and took a deep breath. A strand of hair fluttered across her nose, making her nose itch and she sat back sharply and reached in the backseat for her purse.

"Damn," she muttered, digging through the mess of notes she'd made on napkins, candy wrappers and used envelopes. "Where's my hair clip?"

She finally found a grubby rubber band and scraped her hair back in a ponytail off her neck. Impatiently she turned the key and backed out of the parking place, barely even glancing behind her. She stepped on the gas and sped out of the parking lot.

She needed to find Shane and discuss what to do next about his brother. But as soon as she had that issue out of the way, she planned to ask him how large a part guilt had played in him kissing her. Because his kiss had haunted her all night—even more than her memories of the past.

Maybe if she were more experienced where love and romance were concerned, she'd know how to tell the difference between a pity kiss and one that felt as if she were the woman he'd looked for his whole life. But she wasn't. And she was just insecure enough to worry that Shane's sense of honor and his feelings of guilt were driving this attraction between them.

Her mother was right. If there was something bigger between her and Shane, she needed to find out what it was. She wasn't going to let Adam ruin her life a second time.

CHAPTER TWELVE

TWENTY MINUTES LATER she pulled into Pauline Smith's driveway behind a white SUV that was loaded with suitcases.

"Uh-oh."

Her heart started a frenetic little dance. She didn't know what she'd thought might happen after the way they ended things last night but running away really didn't seem like something a Bernese mountain dog would do.

Shane walked out carrying a box of papers. She recognized some as the notes they'd made during the past week of working together. His laptop was sticking out at an angle, too. Hardly packed properly for an airplane trip.

She got out. "Going somewhere?"

He shoved the box beside his suitcase and walked to her, stopping only to sweep her into his arms and kiss her. She was too surprised to do anything but kiss him back. And suddenly she had her answer. This wasn't about feeling sorry for her. This was about love.

The realization made her push him away. She didn't love him back. She cared for him. She liked him. She lusted after his body. But she couldn't love him. Not after what his brother did to her.

"That wasn't exactly the greeting I was expecting," she said on a ragged breath.

He shrugged. "I saw an opening and took it."

"Well, don't make a habit of it, okay?" When he didn't answer, she repeated her earlier question. "Where are you going?"

"Deadwood. I rented a suite at one of the casinos. You're going, too."

"I beg your pardon? Why would I do that?"

He walked to his car and closed the rear doors. "Because it's the only way to keep you safe. I thought about moving in with you since your mother is gone, but then I opted for a more public venue. Like a lot of politicians, Adam tends to avoid confrontations that would mean intense public scrutiny." He didn't give her time to formulate a reply before he added, "I've got a couple of interviews scheduled with the local press, and I'd like you with me to give the Sentinel Pass perspective."

"Interviews? About what?" Not the rape. She wasn't ready to go public with that.

"*Sentinel Passtime*. And giving you a higher profile will make Adam think twice about hassling you." He paused. "Unless you've already gone to the police. In that case I'm calling a bodyguard service." He dug out his fancy phone.

Bodyguard? "Stop it. You're scaring me."

"Good. I want you to take this seriously, Jenna. My brother is not someone you can afford to underestimate. I don't want to influence your decision. You have to do what's right for you and I'll support you any way I can, but, if you want my opinion—"

"I do, actually. Mostly I get sick to my stomach thinking about reopening the case. But there's a part of me that is appalled by that attitude. He shouldn't get away with what he did."

He took her hand and led her to a small, weathered bench. He brushed off some reddish pine needles and waited for her to sit before joining her. She yanked on the hem of her sea-green shorts, wishing she'd worn something more businesslike.

"I talked to Adam this morning. He offered to pay you money to let it go. No specific amount was mentioned, but he's a very wealthy man, so you could probably name your price."

She sat back, appalled. "God, this just gets uglier and uglier. Now I get to turn into an extortionist?"

"I told him you wouldn't go for that kind of deal."

"What did he say?"

Shane looked at a point over her shoulder. The expression on his beautiful face almost made her cry. "He reminded me of what happens to people who cross him." He shifted his gaze back to her and clasped her shoulders. His hands were warm, but the intensity of his gaze made her shiver. "Jenna, you've got to believe me. My brother is dangerous. I've probably always known it, but in the past I could pretend he was just messing with my head. Not anymore. He more or less admitted that he had something to do with a little girl's death when we were kids."

Jenna bit her lip, her heart aching for him. "What would you do if you were me?"

He let go of her and turned to sit forward, elbows on knees, hands twisting together. In profile, his eyes were narrowed, his expression intense as he stared at the ground. "Make the deal. Move on with your life."

She let out an involuntary cry. "No. You wouldn't say that if you were there that night."

He swung toward her, his brown eyes filled with pain

and compassion. "I *was* there, Jenna. I saw you talking to him across the room and I thought, 'Once again the girl of my choice goes for Joe College.' I don't know how Adam knew I was interested in you—maybe that twin sense is one-sided where we're concerned. If not for me, you probably wouldn't have been his victim."

He blamed himself, she realized in surprise. "Rape is about power, Shane, not sex. He needed someone to dominate, humiliate and crush. I was cocky, flirtatious and full of myself. I'm not saying what happened was my fault. It wasn't. But I can see now where someone like your brother would have seen my attitude as a challenge." She took his hand. "And it wasn't your fault, either. Maybe he's mentally ill or just mean. I don't know, but he has to be held accountable for his actions. Or he'll do it again."

Shane looped a lock of hair that had come loose from her ponytail behind her ear with his free hand. The gesture was tender and sweet, and he smiled in a way that told her he appreciated her letting him off the hook but didn't really believe her that he wasn't at least partly to blame. "I'll do whatever you decide is best for you. But at least let me have some control over the logistics. You'll be with me, or, if you don't want that, I'll hire someone to stay with you twenty-four/seven."

She cocked her head. "You, huh?" She pretended to think about the proposition. "Well…if that's my only option, I guess I'll hang with you at the casino. Will there be gambling?"

He smiled. "Why not? Suddenly, I'm feeling lucky."

She elbowed him playfully. "Oh, really?"

His blush was totally out of character and endearing. "I didn't mean…I…"

She laughed and brushed a quick kiss across his lips. She wasn't a naive little girl anymore, and she sure as hell was nobody's victim. She decided who she wanted to be with and why. Despite all the reasons not to get involved with him, she liked the way he made her feel—alive and smart and valued. Even if nothing long-term could come of it, she was entitled to grab a little gusto while she had the chance.

"So, do I have time to go home and pack a bag?" she asked.

He pulled her to her feet and walked her to her car. "I'll follow you there, then we'll take mine to Deadwood."

As she drove home—with Shane right behind her—she tried to picture what would happen between them once she contacted the authorities in Brookings and got the case reopened. Even if Shane felt no familial loyalty to his brother, Adam's arrest—and his relationship to Shane—would probably make the news.

Her stomach turned over as she pictured the headlines: *Sentinel Passtime* Producer Beds Brother's Rape Victim. The complications could be horrific, but she couldn't *not* do something.

She'd give herself a couple of days to figure out what to do. Once Adam was arrested and Shane knew she was safe, Shane could go back to California and direct the TV pilot. She'd use the money that she earned from scriptwriting to hire a lawyer to make sure justice was served.

She pulled into her driveway, smiling at the white car that stopped a few inches from her bumper. After that, they'd see.

"SWEET," SHE SAID, stepping into the spacious, luxuriously appointed room a couple of hours later. "No pun intended," she added with a chortle.

Shane groaned. "Really awful."

They'd wound up swinging past the Mystery Spot before heading to Deadwood. Everything was fine; the parking lot well over half-filled.

He closed the door behind them, dropping their two bags beside the door of the adjoining bedroom, and looked around. "Not quite what I asked for. Only one bedroom, but I guess we should be thankful they had anything available. Is this town always this busy?"

He set the pair of plastic entry passes on a replica antique table as he moved farther into the room. The motif was early bordello but with modern amenities, like a flat-screen TV inside an armoire. He walked to the ruby velvet sofa and tested it out. "The desk clerk said this makes into a bed, so we'll be okay."

"Uh-huh," she mumbled, strolling into the bathroom. "Oh, my Lord," she cried, "I've died and gone to heaven. Look at this."

The jetted tub was the size of her entire bathroom at home. Clever little battery-operated candles of various sizes were grouped in the far corner. She picked up a tiny bottle from a tray of assorted bath amenities. Ylang-ylang. Not a scent she was familiar with but one she'd been dying to try. She unscrewed the top and sniffed. "Nice."

She checked her watch, then looked over her shoulder at Shane, who was lounging against the door frame watching her. "Did I overhear you make dinner reservations? Do I have time for a soak?"

"Absolutely. I'll set up my laptop and get some work done." He disappeared before she could come up with a clever way to invite him to join her. He'd been nothing but professional ever since he'd assumed the role of bodyguard, which, perversely, she found both annoying and a challenge.

She kicked off her sandals and walked to the opposite end of the tub to open the valves. Hot moist steam rose almost immediately as the bath began to fill. She upended the little bottle under the cascade of water and breathed deeply. The scent was relaxing, yet slightly exotic. Intriguing even.

Returning to her original spot, she drew up her bare feet and rested her back against the tile to watch the tub fill…and pout. *God, I suck at flirtatious banter.*

Although, the thought hit her, she'd held her own when she and Shane were writing dialogue for Cooper's and Libby's characters. Shane had laughed often and praised Jenna for adding an extra kick of spice that he would have missed. She'd credited all the chick-lit romance novels Char had made the book-club members read, but maybe there was some coy, provocative, sex goddess inside her waiting to come out.

Yeah, right. Her snort of laughter made Shane pop his head into the room. He had their two overnight bags in hand. "You okay? There's bottled water in the minibar."

"Right, Midas. And there's a convenience store on the corner that sells the same brand for under a buck," she said dryly. "My father used to say hotel minibars were a sucker's road to perdition."

He disappeared but returned a moment later with a distinctive green bottle of French water in one hand and two champagne flutes in the other. "We're in Deadwood," he said with a wink. "How's the saying go? 'Pray for me. I just left hell and I'm headed to Deadwood'?"

She took the glass, shaking her head. "Not exactly, but

write that down. It sounds like something Coop's character would say."

He filled their glasses and they toasted lightly. The faint
tinkle of crystal raised gooseflesh on her arms.

"You're cold," he said. "I'll close the door behind me."

She spun around on her butt and kicked out one leg,
blocking his exit. "I'd rather you stayed."

He had to double clutch his glass to keep from dropping
it. "Why?"

She rose and set the glass on the marble counter behind
him then leaned into him and looped her arms around his
neck. "You know, for a writer, you seem to lack a certain
amount of imagination."

He locked his fingers together at the base of her spine.
She loved how the weight of his hands naturally brought
her hips to his. "Not so, my sweet coquette. I've been
imagining you in my arms, in my bed, since the first day
I got here. Not even your favorite romance author could
have seen this coming."

"If I told you that speaking French turns me into putty
in your arms, would that give you an unfair advantage?"

He nuzzled her neck and slowly kissed a sensitive spot
below her ear. "I'll take any advantage you give me, but
sadly, I learned most of my French from Pepé le Pew."

She practically doubled over laughing. The release
broke the last of any ice between them. She felt young and
alive and sexy. She quickly turned off the water and
stripped off her T-shirt, shorts and underwear. She didn't
know why she was neither embarrassed nor hesitant.

One foot. Two feet.

"Hot," she yelped, and hopped back out.

Shane quickly gave the cold water lever a turn, then

wrapped his arms around her. "Poor baby. I could kiss your toes, but—"

"Kiss me instead," she said. "I don't know where this newfound lack of inhibition is coming from, but if you're smart you'll make the most of it."

His lips fit with hers as if they'd been two halves of the same whole at some point. But he broke away a few moments later to bend over and test the water. She took advantage of the position to put her hand on his hip. Lean, but sculpted muscle. Black jeans, as usual. "Someone's just a tad overdressed for this pool party. Maybe you don't want to—"

He caught her hand and kept it in place as he turned around. Just the right level to feel proof of his desire.

"I want," he said. "Hop in. The water's perfect. I'll be right back."

Shane hurried into the bedroom. He actually needed a few seconds to collect himself. Everything was moving at the speed of light. In a good way, but he sure as hell didn't want Jenna to have any regrets. The pressure was on to make this as mind-blowingly fabulous as possible.

He looked down at the bulge in his pants. No pressure. Yeah, right, he thought with a rueful grin.

He stripped in the bedroom and unpacked his toiletry kit. He wasn't a player—or a Boy Scout—but he did believe in being prepared. He dug out a small box of high-end condoms, tossing a couple on the bed. From now on he planned to have one in his pocket at all times.

On his way back to the bathroom, he spotted his phone. One missed call. *Tough.* There was only one person he wanted to talk to and she was naked, wet and waiting.

The heady scented steam had increased since he left.

The warmth was nice after the air-conditioning in the outer areas. He hung up the two fluffy robes he'd grabbed on his way past the closet, then closed the door.

"Ah…" she said, paddling through the bubbles to rest her arms on the marble decking around the tub. "I like your suit. Finally, something other than black."

A chuckle rumbled from his belly upward. God, he loved her.

"I spend a lot of time by my pool."

"So I see. And you prefer a Speedo."

He stepped closer. "I usually skinny-dip. Early morning or before bed. But when I'm on the phone or working on the computer, I wear a swimsuit. May I join you?"

She moved aside, but her gaze never left him. "No tattoo," he heard her murmur. "I should have guessed." He didn't know what she was talking about, but he could almost feel the touch of her eyes on his chest, his belly, his groin. He felt a renewed surge of desire that told him he was going to need all his focus to keep from embarrassing himself.

He sank into the water, spreading his legs to the outside of the tub, giving her space in the middle. Her knees were visible, like twin islands in the bubbles as she leaned back opposite him, head against the tiled wall. Her hair was still in a ponytail, leaving her shoulders exposed. With languid grace, she took a sip from the flute he'd given her earlier.

"I'm sorry that's not Dom Perignon."

She polished off the water. "I'm not. I don't want anything to dull my senses. I've waited a long time for this."

He swallowed. "You've never been with anyone since…?"

She stopped him with a toss of her head. "No. I have dated since college. A couple of semiserious relationships, but they didn't gel, so to speak."

"Why not?"

She shrugged. "I think I put too much pressure on them. Maybe I was asking too much at the time."

He wondered what that meant for him, now. "Such as proving to you the male sex isn't made up entirely of jerks?"

She had to lever out of the water to set the glass on the floor. The movement gave him a glimpse of her long, smooth back and a profile of her globe-shaped breast. His throat constricted and he almost forgot to breathe.

She scooted closer, crossing her legs to sit up straight. "I wanted them to make me whole," she said, her fingers spread wide to lightly skim down her body from head to waist. "Finally, I figured out that was my job."

He reached out as reverently as if he were touching a masterpiece by Michelangelo. He brushed the underside of her chin with the back of his fingers then slowly retraced the path her hands had taken. "You look spectacularly complete to me."

She closed her eyes and inhaled invitingly when he reached her breasts. Her flesh filled his palms, her small, ruddy nipples pebbling beneath his touch. He flicked his thumbs back and forth until they were taut then he leaned over and took first one, then the other in his mouth and suckled.

"Oh. Oh, that feels so…nice," she cried.

She cleared the distance between them, water sloshing like a slippery aphrodisiac in every fold and niche. Her ankles tucked in behind him. When they kissed, he tasted traces of bubble bath, a hint of mint from the chewing gum they'd had earlier and…Jenna. Delicious. Intoxicating.

With one hand in his hair and the other behind his back,

she wiggled closer, sending warm waves over his groin driving his need to critical mass.

He knew he needed to slow things down, but his body—and her hands traveling down his sides—seemed to have another agenda.

"I...we...Jenna..." he cried when her fingers angled across his groin. The hot water caressing his penis was bad enough. If Jenna touched him, he might completely lose his edge.

He made an executive decision. Losing control at this point wasn't an option. He stood, taking her with him. Once he was sure she had her balance, he dipped to pick her up and carefully stepped over the side of the tub.

She started to laugh. "Something you don't like about tubs?" she asked, looping her arms around his neck.

"Lack of traction," he said, wiping his feet on a well-placed floor mat. The last thing he wanted was to slip on the tile floor and injure them both. "And beds give us more options. Would you mind grabbing a towel? My hands are full."

She had to stretch over his shoulder to reach the stock of thick white towels. This provided the perfect opportunity to kiss her. She relaxed against him and opened her mouth so his tongue could explore, making sure it didn't miss a spot.

When he felt the texture of the towel against his back, he looked at her and smiled. "We're squeaky clean. Now, we can play as long as we want and we don't have to worry about the water getting cold."

"If we fool around too long, we'll miss our reservations for dinner," she warned.

He opened the door and walked straight to the bed. "There's always room service."

The air temperature was a jolting difference and the trickles of water down his spine felt like icicles.

"My father—" she stopped, a grin making her eyes a lighter shade of green "—isn't paying the bill. Maybe I'll order lobster."

The admission told him more than she probably even realized. The past was then. This was now.

And *now* had never looked better, he thought as he carefully laid her down and used the towel to dry her shoulders, tummy and legs.

Or tasted better.

He licked the underside of her breasts until she squirmed impatiently and let out a small, wordless cry. He understood. He needed more, too.

Jenna kept her eyes closed and focused on the feelings this amazing man was able to create in the most unexpected ways and places. She ran her hands over his body, his smooth, muscular back, and caressed the ample body mass in his shoulders. He was strong and beautiful. His masculine scent blended with the bath oil to create a heady aphrodisiac that blocked any inhibitions she might have had.

She felt like a new person. A whole, undamaged person who wasn't afraid to love completely because she knew she could trust this man implicitly.

A man who used protection without making a big deal about it. A man who worshiped her body so completely that when he entered her she welcomed him without reservation. That had never happened before. No anxious moments, no worrying about freezing up at the wrong instant or not being slick enough. This was happening the way it was supposed to, and she could stop worrying about trying too hard.

"Perfect," he murmured, slowly rocking his hips back and forth. "Jenna, this…is…so…right."

"Yes." *Finally.* And as she responded instinctively to a rhythm that connected on the most basic level of her being, she knew she'd found that lost part of herself again.

CHAPTER THIRTEEN

"OH, MY GOD," JENNA exclaimed hitting the touch pad on the laptop to stop the action on the screen. "She was amazing, wasn't she?"

She tilted her chin to look at the man sitting on the couch beside her. With the one-hour difference between the Hills and the West Coast, they'd had time that morning for a shared shower that more than made up for not making love in the tub the day before, and a leisurely breakfast in bed before Shane needed to set up the link to view Bess's read.

Shane had explained that a casting director had already culled a huge number of potential candidates for the various roles. She'd consulted with him on the top three or four and from that pool two would read for the part. He'd called her mother his "dark horse."

"Incredible," he murmured, scribbling something on his lined pad. "I want to watch it again before we look at any of the others. I had something…" He hunched forward and typed in some command.

Jenna sat back with a sigh. She didn't need to watch it again. Her mother had owned the part. She'd come across as the perfect combination of ditzy and wise. No one else could play this part as well. Of that much Jenna was certain.

She picked up her coffee cup and took a sip of the lukewarm brew as she watched Shane work. She admired the way he was able to hone his focus. She'd received the benefit of that intent attention several times last night.

Rapture of a lost heart found, she'd written in her notebook just before dawn.

She'd slipped out of bed while Shane slept and, wrapped in a slightly damp hotel robe, she'd curled up in this very spot to try to put her feelings on paper. An old habit that she'd fallen into after the rape to rid herself of the fear created by her recurring nightmare.

But last night there'd been no nightmare, no faceless stalker coming after her, faster and faster. She forced down another gulp of coffee and looked at her notebook, resting on the end table a few feet away.

This morning she'd used the familiar cathartic process to document—liberate in a way—the joy and feelings of bliss their lovemaking had aroused in her. She'd poured her feelings into the words, then, instead of hiding the book away, she'd left it open and returned to bed. She'd written:

Imprisoned by a web of scars,
I find my heart liberated at last.
By love.

And she did love him. More than she'd ever dreamed possible. She wasn't sure what that meant, since they hadn't talked about the past…or the future. Adam wasn't a blip on their radar that might suddenly go away. The world—Shane's and hers—was out there waiting, but they remained cocooned in this suite. For a few minutes more.

She glanced at her watch. They needed to leave soon. Even before Robyn had agreed to take over as manager of the Mystery Spot, she'd informed Jenna that she would need this afternoon off. Some kind of out-patient surgery that she'd had scheduled for several months.

Jenna polished off the dregs in her cup, then stood, brushing off crumbs of the croissant she'd nervously inhaled prior to her mother's screen test. "Are you going to offer Mom the part?" she asked, unable to hold in the question any longer.

"Absolutely," Shane answered, closing the laptop. "Is that okay with you? There's no guarantee the show will make the cut next month, but we're going to give it our best shot and she's perfect as Aggie."

A skittery feeling shot through her belly, but that could have been from the caffeine—or due to the look of desire she read on Shane's face. Why had she ever thought he was mysterious and hard to read? She laid her hand on his shoulder. "Sorry, Charlie, I have to go to work."

His lips pulled to one side. "I know. I can't explain it, but apparently I have a thing for women in uniforms. Who knew?"

She looked down at her purple-and-yellow shirt tucked into her khaki Bermuda shorts. "If this turns you on, you're one sick puppy, but I love you."

She choked slightly, realizing too late the flippant admission had slipped out without her planning it. Her cheeks turned hot and she covered them with her hands, peeking through her fingertips. "Oops. I didn't mean that. Well, I did, I think. But not like that. Oh, shoot, I gotta go."

Shane hooted and pulled her to his lap. "Hey, relax. After last night I think it's self-explanatory that we have very deep feelings for each other. The words will start to fit if we give ourselves a little more time."

She let out a sigh. "This is all new to me."

He kissed her tenderly. "Me, too."

Heat flared up instantly, and she wrapped her arms around his neck to deepen the kiss. She loved the taste of him, the shape of his teeth and playfulness of his tongue, but a minute or so later, responsibility reared its ugly head. "Work. Zikes. I have to go."

She jumped up and raced across the room for her purse and backpack. She couldn't pack a lunch, of course, but she'd grab some junk food from the snack bar at the Mystery Spot.

Shane met her at the door, the strap of his laptop case slung over one shoulder. He pulled his dark glasses out of the breast pocket of his black T-shirt and snagged one of the room keys. "Let's go."

She hesitated. "Do you really think this is necessary? I'll be in the midst of dozens of people all day."

His eyes narrowed stubbornly. "You still have to get there and back."

"But we left my car at the house to throw Adam off our trail. If I use your car, he wou—"

He held up his hand to stop her. "This isn't open for discussion, Jenna. I'm going. You can drive. I'll work on the road and once we get to the Mystery Spot, I'll stay in the office. You won't even see me, unless there's a problem."

She gave up with a sigh. "It's the Bernese mountain dog in you, isn't it? Okay. Let's go."

He was true to his word.

THE DAY FLEW BY with very few surprises—unless you counted the catering van that pulled into the parking lot at noon and served an impromptu lunch for the forty-five people present, including tourists from Norway, South Africa and Pennsylvania. Jenna had never tasted a more delicious Chinese chicken salad in her life, and the positive goodwill the gesture generated was probably impossible to calculate. She'd thanked Shane by dragging him into the storage closet for some hot and heavy breathing.

"So, how 'bout I show you a little more of the Hills?" she asked, as they headed home after her eight-hour stint. They'd planned to have dinner at the hotel since they'd missed their reservations the night before.

"Sure. What did you have in mind?"

She put on the blinker, turning the opposite way from the road they commonly took back to the main highway. "There's a back way to Lead and Deadwood. You haven't even seen the Open Cut, have you?"

"What's that?"

Jenna kept her attention on her driving even as she related some of Homestake Gold Mine's glorious and inglorious past. "Now, there's a terrific visitor's center, and you can view the end result of years and years of mining. I can't guarantee we can find a parking place, though. Lead is a popular tourist area in the summer."

When she turned toward Rochford, traffic fell away substantially, although the number of motorcycles picked up.

"It's really gorgeous here," Shane said, lowering his window. "The air smells clean and healthy. And the pace is... I like this."

"Me, too. I missed South Dakota when I lived in

Montana. Don't get me wrong, that's a beautiful state, but the Hills are special. I can't imagine living anywhere else."

She'd spoken from the heart, but when she glanced at him she realized she'd said something wrong. He was frowning again. She started to ask what was bothering him when she noticed a truck behind her. A big, midnight-blue, four-wheel-drive beast that looked like a more modern version of the one Mac drove. It was right on her tail and appeared in a hurry to pass, but on the curving two-lane road, that didn't happen without someone pulling over.

Her heart rate increased and her palms were sweating by the time she spied a spot wide enough for her to ease over. Shane pulled his seat-belt strap away from his chest to twist around and look over his shoulder. At that exact moment, the truck shot ahead as if passing, but failed to move over far enough, striking the Escalade with enough force to send the car straight for the edge of the embankment.

Jenna reacted by slamming on the brakes. She avoided a tree but could do nothing to keep the car's momentum on the gravel shoulder from carrying them straight over the embankment. In what felt like minutes but probably took place in microseconds, the car plunged nose down about five feet, grazing a huge boulder with the passenger-side bumper, which deployed Shane's airbag. His body contorted pretzel-like in the instant before a solid white pillow stopped her from hitting the steering wheel.

Dazed and choking from some sort of dust, all she could hear at first was her heartbeat in her ears. Her mouth hurt and she tasted blood. Moments later a voice said, "This is your OnStar operator. We show that the car's airbags have deployed. What is the nature of your emergency? Do you need an ambulance?"

Jenna forced her eyes open. She turned her chin to look at Shane, slumped awkwardly and unresponsive in the seat beside her. "Yes," she said, somehow finding her voice. "Help. Someone tried to run us off the road. He might still be there. Help."

The shrill cry of her voice echoed in the car, but it was dampened by the sound of the car engine that was still running. She tried to put the car in Park but her right wrist hurt too badly. She twisted across her body to give an extra push with her left hand then she undid her seat belt and opened the door.

Fear and panic followed closely by fury helped her fight through her scattered aches and pains to slide out of the car and hurry around the back to the passenger side. The door was crushed. There was no way she could open it to help Shane out if he regained consciousness.

Feeling light-headed, she looked around, straining to hear the sound of a truck engine. Was Adam waiting nearby to finish them off? If he'd known the road better, he could have chosen a spot to ram them that would have ensured their deaths. They were lucky they crashed where they did. If he figured that out, he'd be back.

She opened the back end of the car and somehow managed to get her hands on the tire iron. Probably a ridiculously futile weapon if he returned, but this time she'd fight him with her last breath. This time she was defending the man she loved, too.

Carrying the heavy weight in her left hand, she returned to the driver's side and crawled in, groaning as new pains came to light. The adrenaline was beginning to dissipate, making her more aware of the results the crash had had on her body.

She put her face close to Shane's. He was breathing, but he still hadn't moved. She closed her eyes and prayed that he'd be okay. He had to be.

SHANE WOKE to a subtle but persistent pounding in his head. Possibly the worst hangover of his life, he decided, once his brain engaged. But when he opened his eyes, he knew instantly what had happened and where he was.

An accident. He'd heard Jenna's cry as they hit something…or had something hit them? He wasn't clear on the details, and only bits and pieces of what happened next filtered through the haze of memory. But he was definitely in a hospital. He'd been there overnight. He remembered waking when a nurse flashed a penlight in his eyes.

She'd told him he was going to be fine and gave him a sip of water to dissolve some of the cotton in his mouth so he could ask about Jenna.

"You mean her?" she'd whispered, stepping to one side so he could see a pile of blankets with a mop of red hair sticking out the top in an armchair. "She hasn't left your side. And apparently she called in reinforcements since there's been a pretty steady parade of people in and out till visiting hours ended."

He slowly turned his head, but the chair was empty. "Shit," he muttered, trying to sit up. If she left the safety of the hospital, Adam might—

"What do you think you're doing? Get back in that bed this instant."

He recognized her voice, but he'd never heard her sound

so stern. "Got that bossy-teacher thing from your dad, right?" he teased, inching sideways to see her.

She rushed to his side. He took a quick assessment of the damage. Butterfly bandage above her eye. Right wrist in a brace of some kind. Slight hitch in her step. But she looked perfect to him. His insides bunched in a tight knot from all the feelings that hit him at once. She could have died. First the rape. Now this. He was a curse.

He fell backward and rolled on his side. The pain was severe, and welcome. "Oh, God, Jenna, I can't believe that happened. I was supposed to keep you safe. Ha," he cried throwing the arm that didn't have the IV over his eyes. "I suck. I should have called in a professional team. Once again I underestimated my brother's depravity."

She pried his arm down, first gently then with force. "Look at me, Shane. I'm fine. This wrist thing is Mom's. I had Char bring it from the house. Nothing's broken, but there might be a slight sprain. This is just to remind me not to use it so much."

He looked at her wrist but couldn't meet her eyes. "You were limping."

"A bruise on my knee. And the cut on my forehead is probably from the airbag deploying. A scratch. The aches and pains are soft-tissue injuries. You're going to feel them, too, once they take you off the good painkillers. But they say you had a slight concussion, so they kept you overnight. Except for a heightened sensitivity to light and maybe a headache if you read too much for the next couple of weeks, you'll make a full recovery, too."

He sighed and closed his eyes. The pain was less than it had been. He craved a shower and food, but other than that he felt pretty good. Surprisingly good.

"Your rental car saved us," she said. "Both literally and figuratively. Side-impact air bags kept your head from hitting the same rock the car sideswiped. And the onboard satellite thingy called for help just seconds after the wreck. The police figured that's why whoever did this didn't come back."

"It was Adam, of course. Did you tell them that?"

She kicked off her shoes and climbed onto the bed, sitting crossed-legged. She'd changed clothes. The dark taupe running suit and bright pink T-shirt was probably a good idea, given the chilly hospital environment. Her hair was pulled back in a loose twist.

"I told them everything. The rape. Your mom's deathbed confession. What Adam told you about hurting a little girl. Everything. This morning an officer came by to take your statement, but I wouldn't let him wake you up. He said Adam had checked out of the Alex Johnson early yesterday morning. They found the truck. It belongs to a Sturgis man. His son, who goes to college at the University of Minnesota, has been driving it to work since he came home for summer break. The father wasn't clear about what kind of work the kid was doing or for whom. His son hasn't been home in a couple of days."

Shane tried to recall any details from the crash but drew a blank. "I can't remember squat. You said something about a truck tailgating us, then—" His pulse sped up until she grabbed his hand.

"Shane," she said briskly to draw his attention. "It's okay. This is out of our hands now. The police have a warrant out for the kid for leaving the scene and attempted murder. If they find him, he'll give up your brother, assuming, of course, that Adam paid him to do it. If Adam was behind the wheel, then the police will make a case against him. The cop told me they'd taken fingerprints from the truck, and they were even going to the Mystery Spot to see if any of the prints match this guy. They think he might have been working for Adam for some time."

Shane blinked in surprise. That connection had never crossed his mind. He turned his hand palm up to interlace his fingers with hers. His heart rate was almost back to normal and the metallic taste in his mouth was lessening. "Can I have some water?"

She scooted off the bed and poured him a glass. "Are you hungry?" she asked. "The nurse said we could get a tray whenever you woke up."

He swallowed the cool liquid gratefully and nodded, wincing slightly at the echoing chain of pain the motion set off. She leaned close and kissed him. "Easy there, sparky. Small movements. I'll order your breakfast."

He closed his eyes to rest while she was gone. What seemed like seconds later, he smelled the arrival of a tray and opened his eyes to see someone he vaguely recognized deposit it on his bedside table.

"Hi. I'm Kat. We sorta met at the wedding. I'm one of the book-club members. Jenna's in the lobby talking to a detective and she asked me to make sure you got this."

He placed her as soon as she said her name. She had two sons. They'd accompanied her to the wedding. He remembered thinking she looked too young and innocent to be the twice-divorced mother of two, but up close he could see a certain ageless wisdom in her eyes. "Thank you," he said, trying to sit up.

"Let me do that." She grabbed a remote control of some sort and punched a button, making the head of his bed raise up. "I used to work in a hospital. Back when I thought I wanted to be a nurse. Emptying bedpans cured me of that idea in a hurry," she added with a wink.

She removed the plastic warming covers and opened a sealed bag of eating utensils, setting everything within reach and handing him the paper napkin.

"Where are your children?"

Her smile changed her from pretty to beautiful. "One's with his dad and the other is taking a summer arts program put on by the college where I go to school. I'm finishing up a minithesis for one class this summer, then I'm sched-uled to student teach this fall. That means I was available to run by the hotel and pack up your stuff when Jenna asked. She gave me the key. I moved everything to Libby's."

Even though he felt funny eating in front of a stranger, his hunger got the better of him and he attacked the sur-prisingly fluffy mound of scrambled eggs. Even devoid of seasoning, which he didn't bother taking the time to apply, they weren't bad. "Why there?" he mumbled between bites.

She slathered a glob of purple jelly on a triangle of toast and gave it to him. "Coffee black or with artificial, hydrogenated white stuff?"

He grinned. "You make that sound so appealing. I'll have mine straight, thanks."

"Good choice." She passed him the cup. "Um...why Libby's? Jenna called Cooper and Lib. They're on their way back. Libby suggested you and Jenna stay in the guest house. Libby's brother lives right next door, and he's... well, nobody messes with Mac."

"Okay."

She smiled. "Good. I'm glad that's decided." She paced around restlessly a few moments, checking her watch. "She should be here by now. I'm going to go check. I know it's silly to worry. She was with a cop, right? But, it's the mother in me. I'm neurotic. Just ask my sons." She was halfway out the door when Jenna appeared. Kat practically wilted with relief.

The two of them spoke softly a few seconds, then Kat leaned back into the room to say goodbye. "Gotta dash. Get better soon." She wiggled her fingers at him, then disappeared.

Jenna came toward the bed considerably more slowly than her high-octane friend.

"I like her. She's interesting."

"Should I be jealous?"

He pushed the portable table away and made a place for her to sit. "I've been in love with you ever since college, Jenna. I didn't realize that until a few days ago, but you've always been in my heart. For most of that time you were a ghost of an ideal woman whose life would have been different if I'd done something. Not that I knew what that was or how I could have prevented what happened to you, but you were always in the back of my mind. And then, when my mother told me about Adam, you were in the front of my mind. Wrapped up in a neat little ribbon of guilt. And now I nearly got you killed."

She shook her head. "I hate it that you keep taking the blame for your brother's actions. The cops better hope they find Adam before I do. He's got a screw loose, okay? This isn't your fault. You're his brother, not his maker."

The food he'd consumed settled heavily in his belly.

"But we're identical twins, Jenna. We came from the same egg. We have almost matching DNA. What if that propensity for evil is in my genes? What if I were to pass it along to future generations? At this point, the world's lucky. Neither of the Ostergren brothers has found a woman willing to bear his child."

An image of his mother admitting that she'd given birth to a monster suddenly filled the all-too-receptive screen in his head. What if he and Jenna had a child like Adam? The anguish would kill her. As it had his mother. He'd be responsible for killing the woman he loved.

The only other alternative was to remain childless. Or adopt. But Jenna deserved everything wonderful that life had to offer—including a little red-haired child with laughing green eyes and a sweet disposition—without worrying if that first tantrum might foreshadow some terrible personality flaw.

The pain in his head blossomed into a black pressure that moved downward toward his lungs. He had to breathe shallowly to keep from gasping like a fish out of water.

"Shane? Look at me. Are you okay?"

He couldn't bear to see the worry on her face that he heard in her voice. The same worry he'd always known was in his mother's heart. "Headache," he choked out.

"I'll call the nurse," she said, squeezing his hand supportively.

The nurse came in and made some kind of adjustment on his IV. The drug it was delivering into his vein worked fast. His panic started to recede, but he still couldn't bear to look at Jenna and see everything he knew he was going to have to give up, so he lay still and pretended to fall asleep.

She leaned close and brushed her lips across his cheek,

then whispered, "I came to tell you that I'll be gone about an hour."

His eyes flew open and he started to protest. "It isn't safe. Where are—"

She put her finger on his lips. "Relax. Rest now. I have a police escort waiting in the lobby. They picked up the college student I told you about and they want to see if I recognize him from the Mystery Spot. The nurse said your doctor should be making rounds within the hour. If they release you today, I want you to promise you won't try to leave until I get back, okay?"

He still didn't feel good about her going somewhere without him. Then the irony struck him. Not only had he failed to protect her, he planned to leave as soon as he was able. But he couldn't abandon her as long as his brother was a threat. "The car—"

"Was totaled, but I called Mac. He brought my car here and parked it in the lot." She fished a set of keys out of her purse and jiggled them. "As soon as you're released, I'm taking you to Libby's. With friends around, Adam wouldn't dare try anything."

Once she was gone, he closed his eyes and tried to sleep, but images he didn't want to see kept rolling on the closed loop in his brain. Jenna at the party—bubbly and animated while flirting with his clean-cut brother. Then, just a couple of days later, sitting in the backseat of her of parents' car. Shattered and lost. Adam at their mother's funeral. Staring at Shane as if trying to guess whether or not she'd divulged his awful secret. Jenna behind the wheel as the car was forced off the road.

Adam was right about one thing. Shane's coming here had been completely self-serving. Maybe if he'd been honest with himself and admitted that he'd been in love with her from the first moment he saw her, he might have been strong enough to do the noble thing and stay away.

Now he had no choice but to leave. Jenna deserved a hell of a lot more than he had to give her. Children, of course, and a chance to raise them in the kind of place where she grew up, not in the hectic, demanding chaos of smog-bound L.A. She'd be better off with someone like Libby's brother. And he planned to tell her that as soon as she got back.

He squeezed his eyes tight and clenched his fists against the pain that surged once again in his head. He knew this was a minor discomfort compared to the anguish he was going to feel after he did the right thing and told her goodbye.

CHAPTER FOURTEEN

"NO, DAMMIT, I didn't recognize him," she told Libby while she waited on a bench outside the police station. She'd collected all her and Shane's personal belongings from the damaged rental car, which was still being held as evidence. Her stomach had nearly emptied when she saw the mangled mess of the front end.

To her vast surprise, she'd discovered Shane's phone still had a charge, so she'd punched in Coop's name and Libby had answered.

"We're making good time because my husband has a lead foot," she said, a loving lilt in her voice. "We should be home in a few hours. Mac said Kat delivered your things to Gran's cabin. Good. You'll be safe in Sentinel Pass."

Safe, but what good was that going to do her when the love of her life was convinced he shared the same genes as a psychopath? Jenna had been near tears ever since she left the hospital, and the disappointment of not ever having seen the skinny blond kid the police had hoped she could identify was galling. The guy had admitted to breaking into the Mystery Spot and even took responsibility for damaging the water main a few weeks earlier. He said he'd been contacted at his MySpace page by a guy he never met. The mystery man paid him to play some harmless pranks on the owners of a business that was obviously a rip-off.

"The police believe Adam is on his way back to Minnesota," Jenna told Libby. "He'll lawyer up, and even if the police can make a connection from the Internet, which isn't likely, Adam would probably claim the kid was a stalker or something."

"Who was behind the wheel of the truck that drove you off the road?"

Jenna sighed. She was tired—physically and emotionally. "The kid claims the truck was stolen, so it was probably Adam. But he must have worn gloves. No prints, except the kid's and his father's."

"Bummer. Cooper wants to know how Shane is doing."

"Good. He might be getting his walking papers as we speak. I'm just waiting for my ride. I—" She glanced up, sensing another presence. She assumed it was the same female cop who had escorted her to the station. Officer Hardgrave. But it wasn't. It was a man with a small, silver gun pointed straight at her.

"Hello, Adam," she said, hopefully loud enough for Libby to hear.

He took the phone from her hand and tossed it into the bushes. "Let's go."

A thousand things flashed through her head. Panic and fear fought for control, but before she could move, a strange and marvelous calm dropped over her like a shield. Everything she'd learned in her self-defense classes funneled down to a tight focus.

Never get in a car with an attacker.
Go limp.

Shout. Make a scene. Be noticed.

Find the sweet spot and strike. Surprise can be your best friend.

She stood and took one step away from the bench to give herself room to maneuver. She instantly assessed the distance between his gun hand and her, and without really even thinking, she rocked back on her left heel and kicked with her right. Gut level, but the impact sent the gun flying.

She went down, too, but was on her feet before he could recover his breath. She didn't stick around to see if he picked up the gun. She ran as fast as her legs would carry her toward a group of strangers approaching on the sidewalk. "Gun," she cried, pointing behind her. "That man has a gun. He's trying to kidnap me."

She wasn't sure exactly what happened next, but one of the people in the crowd—a man in civilian dress—separated himself from the others and drew a weapon. Several shots were fired. Women screamed. Someone knocked Jenna to the ground. She covered her head and pulled her body into a ball to provide the smallest target possible, but within seconds it was over.

The only person injured took a bullet to the chest and died before the EMTs could arrive. His name was Adam Ostergren. A politician from Minnesota, who made the bad decision to pick up his gun when told not to and pointed it at an armed undercover cop with sniper training.

"GOOD GRIEF. I leave for three lousy days and all hell breaks loose."

Shane's eyes flew open at the sound of the familiar voice. "Coop." Shane had been dressed and waiting for what felt like hours for Jenna to return from the police station. Apparently the magic elixir in his IV, which was no longer attached to his arm, he noticed, had knocked him out again. "What are you doing here? You're supposed to be on your honeymoon."

His tall blond friend walked straight to the bed and gave him the once-over. "You look like crap, man. Good thing it's not your mug the audience wants to see or our show would be screwed."

His famous smile turned downward and his hand shook a little when he reached out to place it on Shane's shoulder. "Seriously, Reynard, this sucks. When Jenna called my wife— God, I love saying that," he added with a grin. "My wife started throwing things in the bag and ordering me around. Sheesch. I think we were on the road in like five minutes."

"Why? I'm fine. Little conk on the head. The doctor said I'd probably have some extrabad headaches for a few weeks, but no long-term effects."

Cooper squeezed his shoulder supportively and stared into his eyes for a few seconds. About five seconds too long. That's when Shane knew something was wrong. Seriously wrong.

He brushed aside Coop's hand and swung his feet over the side of the bed to sit upright. "What's going on? Tell me."

"Um...Libby's with Jenna at the police station and they thought you'd be getting anxious to leave and wondering what happened to her so here I am."

Shane pointed to his shoes, sitting by the wheelchair an orderly had brought in anticipation of Shane's exit. That had been—he looked at the clock on the wall—three hours earlier. "Something happened. Is she okay? Adam came back. He found her. But she was with the police. She should have been safe."

Coop raked his fingers through his hair and let out a groan. "She's fine. Honestly. I saw her. They were finishing up some paperwork, then Libby's taking her home. Jenna sent me here to talk to you because she knew you'd be worried." He frowned. "She said she called the hospital and left a message with the nurse. Didn't they tell you?"

Shane squeezed the bridge of his nose waiting for the pounding in his head to lessen. The doctor had also told him to take things easy and avoid stressful situations. Shane had joked that the man obviously had never produced a television show before.

"Yes. I don't remember exactly…something about my brother being spotted. Did they arrest him?"

"Um…he's dead, Shane. I'm sorry to have to tell you that, but he pointed a gun at a cop and they took him out. No one can figure out why he was there. He would have been home free if he'd split, like everyone thought he did. They didn't have any real evidence against him, but he must have snapped. He came back for Jenna and she refused to play the victim."

Shane closed his eyes. He didn't need a great imagination to picture how the drama unfolded. Poor Jenna. Under attack again. But this time she fought back. His chest swelled with pride, but another emotion pressed down on him, making it hard to breathe.

"Jenna thought I should be the one to tell you. She feels responsible, even though none of this was her fault. Lib calls it survivor guilt."

Shane understood what that felt like all too well.

"Are you okay, man? Should I call the nurse?"

"No. I'm fine. Just give me a minute."

Coop pulled up a padded chair and sat. "I know this has to be a shock, buddy. I'm sorry."

Shane shrugged. "Adam and I haven't spoken in years. He was a complete jerk most of the time we were growing up. Self-absorbed and demanding. But Jenna made me remember that it wasn't all bad."

They sat in silence a few minutes, then Shane sighed and scratched the bandage at his temple. If he thought about what was coming, he'd be tempted to crawl back in bed and pull the blanket over his head. A funeral. Sorting out his brother's estate. "Has the press found out?"

Coop nodded. "There were a couple of local affiliates at the police station. That's another reason Jenna isn't here. She figured they'd make the connection soon enough without her leading them to you."

"Where's my laptop? I should compose some kind of statement."

Coop's sigh was so weighty and full of opinion Shane had no choice but to ask, "What?"

Coop kicked Shane's shoes closer to the bed. "Here's what's going to happen and if you give me any crap, I'll sic my wife on you. I'm taking you to Sentinel Pass. You and Jenna will disappear for a few days until that goose egg on your head goes down. Your whack-job brother can hang in the morgue until you're ready to deal with all that. The rest of us will keep the press at bay."

When Shane tried to stand up, the room started to spin and the remains of the breakfast Kat had served him surged upward. He blindly crammed his bare feet into the sandals, fighting the dizziness that sent yellow and black spots across his vision. He almost smiled because the sensation reminded him of the Mystery Spot.

Once he was on his feet he looked at Cooper and said, "Sorry, pal. That was plan A. And it made sense when Jenna and I were…when we had a future. But we don't. Therefore, you'll take me to the nearest hotel. There's one downtown, right? Where my brother stayed. It'll do. I figure a day or two at the outside then I can head home. I have a show to produce and time is running out."

Coop looked like a disappointed child told he couldn't go to Disneyland. "But you and Jenna— Libby and I thought— She sounded so happy before— God, I hate it when my scriptwriter gives me unfinished sentences," he said, making a face. "Will you at least tell me why you're running away? Libby's going to want an answer."

Shane took a deep breath and let it out slowly. "Tell her I'm doing this for Jenna's sake. Jenna deserves a complete life, not the kind she'd have with me." He shuffled unsteadily to the wheelchair. "I think she's suffered enough at the hands of the Ostergren brothers, don't you?"

"The who?"

Shane shook his head and smiled. As his pal had intended. Cooper knew exactly what Shane meant.

"I know it's a lot to ask, Coop, but I'd appreciate it if you and Libby would do your best to convince Jenna to let me slip away without some highly charged emotional confrontation. Tell her my doctor ordered complete rest or something."

Before Cooper could say anything, the nurse arrived with some papers for Shane to sign. Minutes later they were waiting for the elevator, making small talk about possible side effects and what Shane should look for in case he developed a bleed in his head.

The distraction was welcome. It took his attention away from the ache in his heart. His brother was dead, but in a perverse way that Adam would have loved, he'd succeeded in ruining any hope Shane had for a normal, happy life.

In the end, Adam won.

CHAPTER FIFTEEN

SHANE LOOKED OUT THE window of the tiny plane that was taking him to Denver to catch a jet for home. The view was on the wrong side of the plane. He couldn't see the mountains he'd come to love.

Less than two full weeks had passed since he first arrived in this most unlikely of paradises, but his heart had been heavy saying goodbye to Coop and Libby today because he knew he'd never return. Even if the pilot was picked up and the show went into production, he'd hire the limited amount of site work that had to be done. He'd stay on as producer, but new writers and a director would take over.

Coop wouldn't like that, but he'd understand. He'd been there with Shane the past four days, helping him tie up all the loose ends surrounding his brother's death. Fortunately, Shane had been saved having to plan or participate in a funeral because Christina, his stepmother, showed up on Thursday to claim the body.

"The Vampire Queen of St. Paul," Coop had called her.

She blew in on a cloud of Chanel, threatening a wrongful death suit against the Pennington County Sheriff's Department and trying to stir up some support for her cause. She found none. There were too many witnesses. And after a conversation with the Brookings District Attorney who implied that he now had enough evidence to prove that Adam raped Jenna in college thanks to the DNA sample that matched the tissue collected from under Jenna's fingernails at the time of the rape, she shut up and went home, taking Adam's body with her.

Shane had spent most of his time holed up in the hotel room, which wasn't as spacious and memorable as the one he'd shared with Jenna. But he figured that was just as well since he was in mourning—for Jenna, not for his brother.

Late one night, with the help of a bottle of Gray Goose, he'd come to the conclusion that he'd lost his brother years earlier. He'd even written an imaginary dialogue of what he should have said to Adam following their mother's funeral.

"Mom told me I was born by emergency C-section twenty minutes after you because the umbilical cord was wrapped around my neck, like a noose. A part of me has always believed that you somehow did that. In the womb. I don't know how, but even then you wanted it all."

Adam would have laughed or shrugged. He hadn't cared what anyone thought. Possibly, their father's opinion counted for something, but maybe that was because Dad could give Adam the connections he wanted in politics. Shane would never know. He'd probably never understand what drove his brother, who was brilliant in a way. After all, he'd lived a completely amoral life yet still won the respect of many. No doubt that admiration had to do with the image of power he projected. And in the end that feeling of omnipotence, of being above the law, was what had gotten him killed.

Coop didn't agree with Shane's theory. He believed that Adam came back for Jenna because he was fixated on writing the ending his way.

"The guy hated loose ends. You saw the file his assistant sent," Coop had argued. "He'd kept tabs on Jenna ever since college."

From what the detective investigating the shooting had told them, the police believed that Cooper's arrival in Sentinel Pass was what prompted Adam to hire a kid off his alma mater's Web site to make trouble for Jenna. "The fact that Mr. Lindstrom was getting involved with Ms. Murphy's best friend probably set off some kind of alarm bells in your brother's head," the cop had said during a briefing the day before. "The shrink we consulted said your brother probably hoped the distraction would keep Jenna too busy to notice any of Cooper's friends who might show up."

"Like Shane," Coop put in. "What I don't get is how he knew Shane would even remember her. I mean, the rape happened a long time ago and Shane and Jenna weren't exactly an item in college, right?"

The cop didn't have an answer for that, so Shane had supplied his own personal theory. "Adam was pretty intuitive where I was concerned. He must have guessed that I was attracted to her because he went out of his way to make sure I saw him flirting with her. Why that escalated to rape, I have no idea. But I guarantee that neither of us ever forgot that night. By making trouble for Jenna, he was probably just covering all bases."

After the detective left, Shane and Cooper had a serious face-to-face about what was happening with the show. Shane had tried to reassure his friend that the show was on track. "Believe it or not, everything that's happened—right down to the attempt on Jenna's life—fits in the script. Instead of my brother as the bad guy, though, I'm using your mother's crazed bookie. And, naturally, it's you and Libby who get forced off the road, and Libby who winds up in the hospital."

Coop's look of horror hadn't been an act.

"Trust me, Coop. This is good stuff. High drama and great conflict because it drives home the fact that you're a detriment to this woman's life. Thanks to you, her town hates her and a madman has tried to kill her. Obviously, your only option is to leave."

Coop hadn't liked that scenario one bit, but in the end, Shane managed to convince him that a true hero would put the safety and welfare of the woman he loves above his own needs and desires. And after writing the scene in script form, Shane was able to put his laptop aside and compose a letter to Jenna. Longhand.

He tried to pour every ounce of regret he felt for all the damage he and his brother had inflicted on her life. He also confessed how deeply he felt about her and that he would love her for the rest of his life, which was why he needed to leave now, without seeing her again.

You deserve so much more than I can give you. But no one will ever love you as much as I do. Please believe that I only want the very best for you.
Love always, Shane.

The letter, which he'd asked Cooper to deliver—along with Jenna's turquoise hair clip that he'd been carrying in his pocket since that first day at the Mystery Spot—was the last of his loose ends in the Black Hills. Now he was free to go home and make a success of this show—his final way of making things up to Jenna.

As the plane began to climb, it banked west. He leaned his head against the glass, trying to spot some familiar landmarks. The fire lookout on Harney Peak. The big blue reservoir that was Jenna's retreat. He tried to picture her sitting there, pen and paper in hand. He imagined she'd be sad at first, but eventually she'd find Mr. Right—maybe Libby's brother—and have a couple of kids.

And he'd be back in la-la land, doing his thing. He honestly couldn't wait to breathe a little smog. Maybe it would kill him—sooner rather than later.

"I GOT MY PERIOD," Jenna cried. Her cheeks were on fire from blurting out such a personal revelation in front of the entire Wine, Women and Words book club, but she was too upset to care.

The group had convened right after church to accommodate Kat's schedule. Her sons, Tag and Jordie, looking all spit-shined and cute, were out front in Libby's yard, tossing a ball around with Coop, who was trying to learn how to do "Dad things."

"Why couldn't what happened to you happen to me?" she asked Libby, who quite possibly was already starting to show a little baby bump.

"Did you use protection every time?" her ever-practical friend asked.

Jenna nodded. "And I'm on the pill, too."

Libby's mouth dropped open. "Then what you're really asking for is an immaculate conception. I've heard of it happening, but it's pretty rare."

Jenna smiled despite her tears. "I know I'm not making any sense. I really shouldn't be complaining. Mom's happy and healthy. There's money in the bank. And, did I tell you what happened Friday night? We were just getting ready to close the Mystery Spot and these trucks pulled up with huge spotlights, a couple of giant roller machines and enough blacktop to do the entire parking lot. With stripes and official handicap parking spaces and everything."

"Shane?" Kat asked.

"Of course. But when I called the next morning to thank him, the desk clerk at the Alex Johnson said Shane had checked out." She tossed up her hands in frustration. "He sends me this beautiful, almost poetic 'Dear Jenna' letter, but he doesn't have the cajones to face me one last time before leaving for California."

"What a jerk," Char muttered, punching her fist into her palm. Her hair—still sporting light green highlights—was sticking up in places, making her look as if she'd just rolled out of bed. Which she probably had. "I'd like to toss him off the top of Bear Butte."

"But he seemed so sweet and genuine," Kat cried. Her simple denim sundress made her look about sixteen. "Am I the only one who got sucked in by his swoo? Well, aside from Jenna, of course. I was just collateral damage compared to her."

Libby pounded the floor with the talking stick. "This isn't helping, people. I called this emergency meeting of the book club to come up with a strategy to pull Jenna out of the black hole she's let herself slide into. I'm not going to sit by and watch her slowly turn into her mother, who apparently is having too much fun in California to come home and be with her daughter in her time of need."

Jenna rolled her eyes. "Mom stayed in L.A. because I begged her to. She's found an agent and is already getting calls for some bit parts. Possibly even a commercial. I'm not about to do what my dad did and sabotage Mom's big chance. She knows nothing about what happened between Shane and me—the good or the bad. And I plan to keep it that way," she added sternly.

"Where's she staying?" Char asked.

"At Cooper's house in Malibu. Mom said she goes walking on the beach every day and she's never felt healthier." She smiled, picturing her once illness-infatuated mom drinking smoothies and power walking on the sand. "Apparently Coop's neighbor is completely taken with her, but she claims he's too old for her."

"Rollie is who Coop wanted to invite to our wedding but couldn't reach in time," Libby added. "Apparently he was in the hospital for some minor health scare. His doctor has made him clean up his act, Coop said." She looked at Jenna. "You could go to California with us, you know. See your mom. Confront Shane."

"Yeah," Char said, swiping her hands together as if it was a done deal. "Visit your mom, then while you're in the neighborhood, you could drop by Shane's to give him a piece of our minds."

Jenna started to laugh. She wasn't the kind of person who made spontaneous trips halfway across the country on a whim. Her friends knew that. But within seconds Jenna could see that the others were taking the idea seriously.

"What's keeping you here?" Kat asked. "The Mystery Spot is doing better than ever thanks to all the free publicity. And the girl you have managing the place is awesome, right?"

Jenna nodded. "Theoretically, I *could* go. But why would I? In his letter, Shane made it very clear he doesn't want anything to do with me. Can you picture anything more humiliating than throwing myself at a man who rejects me, not once, but twice?"

Libby rocked back in her father's chair. "Well, yes, actually. You could have had your mistake turned into a television show for millions of people to laugh at each week."

She leaned the talking stick against the wall, then looked at Jenna. "Cooper and I were at the airport when Shane left. Even given the fact that he'd been in an accident and lost his brother, he looked like a soul on the fast track to hell. He's hurting, Jenna. And so are you." Tears appeared in her eyes and immediately started to trickle down her cheeks.

"Hormones." She sniffled, reaching for the box of tissues Jenna had needed earlier. "Coop and I both think you should come with us. You can use your mother as an excuse if you want to save face, but we're both concerned about Shane. We think you might be the only person who can shake him out of his depression."

Jenna shot to her feet. "Damn it, Lib, the guy has a right to be depressed. He's lost his entire family. *And* his identical twin turned out to be a genuine psychopath. If Shane's not entitled to mope, who is?"

Kat cleared her throat tentatively and said, "Um…I'm no expert, but I've taken several courses in psychology. And I don't think Adam fits the classic definition of psychopath. He was definitely amoral and destructively self-focused, but he wasn't a Jeffrey Dahmer. From what you've said about Shane's family life, I think his father might have been a big part of Adam's problem."

Char chugged a swig of coffee, then set her mug down with an emphatic snap. "Well, I consulted a shaman about this. We don't call them medicine men anymore," she added, "but this guy sees things we ordinary people can't. Dead-on spooky stuff with amazing accuracy. So, I told what little I know about Shane and Adam and asked him how one twin could turn out normal while the other did really bad things."

She paused for dramatic effect, looking at each of them to make sure they weren't scoffing. "And he said that while these two were born to the same mother, they are not brothers. Their paths have crossed many times in previous lives…as mortal enemies."

She squinted slightly as if trying to recall the shaman's exact words. "Shane might have been the lawman who hunted down Adam and hung him from a tree. Or they could have been soldiers who killed each other in combat. That might explain how they entered the unconscious stream at the exact same moment and wound up sharing a womb." She made it sound so simple and plausible. "The shaman stressed that this was a fluke. They *definitely* are not half of the same whole."

Jenna knew that. She'd known it before she spent the night in Shane's arms, but getting him to believe it was a task beyond her abilities. She wasn't a shaman. Or a psychiatrist. How could she make him see himself as she saw him? As a big, lovable Bernese mountain dog who would sacrifice his own happiness to ensure that she had a wonderful, whole life—complete with kids.

Bernese mountain dog. She inhaled sharply, causing her friends to look at her in alarm. "When I talked to Mom yesterday she said she'd just run into a woman walking two

Bernese mountain dogs on the beach. The lady said the female was from Switzerland but the male came from a breeder in Bakersfield."

"So?" Libby asked.

"So, I know what I have to do." Jenna smiled for the first time since that horrible day in front of the police department. "Your intervention worked," she said, getting up to hug each of her friends. "Libby, I'm going to California with you and Coop. I need to see a man about a puppy."

CHAPTER SIXTEEN

SHANE'S HEAD POUNDED with what had become an all-too-familiar pattern in the ten days since he'd left South Dakota. He'd run out of prescription painkillers a week ago and hadn't bothered contacting his primary physician despite the fact that the debilitating headaches came with predicable regularity morning, noon and night.

Allergies, he thought, closing the patio door on the backyard oasis he loved. Maybe he'd invest in a whole-house air purifier. He'd stay cooped up inside like Michael Jackson or Howard Hughes.

But the more likely culprit, he knew, was stress. He'd had to deal with a ton of it since his return. He'd learned to juggle his PDA and iPhone like hot potatoes. He got more e-mail every day than the damn government. And, unfortunately, the press had decided his brother's sordid story did indeed make for good copy. Not that they knew all the details, thank God, but that didn't stop them from speculating.

Especially about Jenna. Which meant he saw her beautiful face on every tabloid news show and supermarket scandal sheet.

Jenna—the woman Coop wouldn't stop talking about. He'd just arrived to go over his lines for rehearsal the next day.

"Libby and Jenna are like this home makeover tag team. Jenna's got a notebook that she carries everywhere, and every time Libby says something like 'Good Lord, look at the size of his vodka bottle,' she writes it down," Coop said, pacing between the kitchen and the family room bar where Shane was standing. "She's not working for you, right? So what's with the notes?"

Shane almost smiled. Coop's house had been the party place for many years, and a liberally stocked bar was probably the least of Coop's problems where Libby was concerned. He didn't know why Jenna was taking notes, but he could imagine why she found the whole thing amusing.

"So, Bess and Jenna are both living with you?" he asked, adding a banana to the blender. He'd been working on making a smoothie before Coop had shown up.

"Yes, although Bess has an agent now, and she's gone a lot," Coop said, plopping down on a stool. "Talk about hitting the ground running, that woman is going for it, man. Did I tell you she's up for a cosmetics commercial? They're thinking it could turn into something big if *Sentinel Passtime* is a hit."

Shane put the lid on the blender and punched the switch. Neither spoke until Shane was done emptying the contents into two glasses. He added a straw to one glass and passed it to Coop.

Coop took a drink. "Um. Good. Since when did you start eating so healthy? Wait. Don't tell me. Jenna rubbed off on you. I swear she and her mother are more Californian than we are."

Shane stuck a straw in his glass and took a long draw before turning to the sink to rinse out the glass carafe. He'd actually talked to Bess a couple of times since getting home. She'd called to express her sympathy for his loss. She'd also left him with the impression that her daughter hadn't mentioned anything to her mother about their one night together.

Just as well, Shane thought. Still, he was a little surprised. Jenna and Bess had seemed close. He hoped his actions hadn't done something to change their relationship. One more thing to feel guilty about.

"Can I get you anything else?" Shane asked, carrying his glass to the low table beside the buff leather sofa. "I'm gonna take it easy while you read." He sank onto a cushion and kicked out his feet.

Coop took another drink, almost draining the glass, then set it aside. "No, thanks. I'm good. Libby and Jenna and Bess are meeting me and Rollie at Rollie's favorite restaurant for dinner later. I'd offer to add you to the reservations but since you haven't left the house since you got back—"

"Not true. I've been on the set every day."

"I meant socially."

Shane changed the subject. "What did you do for the Fourth of July?" Coop and Libby, along with Jenna, had returned on Wednesday, which had given Coop just one day to meet the other cast members and do a very casual read before the holiday, which fell on Friday. Now he was here on a Sunday trying to play catch-up.

Coop shrugged. "Same as usual."

In the past, they hung out on the beach together, with maybe a dozen or so of Coop's friends around, to watch fireworks from Coop's deck. He understood why he hadn't been invited to this year's gathering—Jenna was there. Still, his feelings were a little hurt.

"What'd you do?" Coop asked, not bothering to glance up from the script.

"Took a painkiller and went to bed early."

"Hmm."

Shane wondered what Jenna thought of L.A. The urge to call her was probably what was fueling his headache, but he was determined to stay strong. Yet, he couldn't stop himself from asking, "How is she?"

Coop lowered the bound set of pages he was holding. "Jenna? Great. She loves the beach. She and Lib are madly converting my old workout room into a nursery slash temporary guest room for Auntie Jenna."

"I thought I was going to be Uncle Shane to the kid."

Coop cocked his head in confusion. "You are. Did you want to be his or her aunt, instead? Is there something you're trying to tell me? Like maybe you're switching teams? Oh, God, is that the real reason you and Jenna broke up? You're gay?"

Shane made a vice of his hands and squeezed his head, hard, to keep it from exploding...until he spotted his friend's devilish grin.

He let out a sigh. Maybe if he saw her, he thought—just to make sure for himself she was okay—his headaches would go away. One less thing to worry about, right?

"What time is your reservation? Maybe Libby and Jenna could drop by here for a drink before you have to leave," Shane heard himself suggest.

Coop's attention was back on the page. "Can't. They're in Bakersfield."

"What's in Bakersfield?"

"Excellent question." Coop's head popped up, trademark grin in place. "Same one I asked. Do you know what my wife told me? That I was on a need-to-know basis, and I didn't need to know. Doesn't that sound like something her character would say?" His smile turned pensive. "Women speak their own language and I'm not bilateral."

Shane bit down on his lip. He didn't know if Coop was trying to make him smile or not, but some of the funk that had been following him around lifted. Jenna was here. She and Libby were doing things, and that was good. She wasn't sitting home feeling sorry for herself, the way he was.

Cooper walked to the manly looking Bogart chair across from him and sat. He hunched forward, his brow knit. "I like Jenna. And her mom is a hoot. But Libby and I have only been married for two weeks. And I know I'm supposed to be working. That's why I'm here with you instead of home in bed with my wife, but I couldn't be in bed with her anyway because she drove to Bakersfield this morning on a secret mission. And apparently I'm persona non loopus because they think I'd tell you."

"Tell me what?"

"If I knew, I'd tell you. See? They're right. I can't be trusted."

Shane rubbed his temple and closed his eyes. What did it matter where Jenna was or what she was doing? He'd walked away from her and the love she'd given so freely. But love came with strings. He'd always known that, and he wasn't about to let her get bogged down in his.

No, they wouldn't meet for drinks or lunch. They wouldn't see each other and pretend everything was okay. Because it wasn't. It would never be okay again because he couldn't marry the woman he loved. Hell, he barely managed to hug Libby goodbye when he left Rapid City, and she was the nicest woman in the world, next to Jenna. But she was also pregnant, and he was never going to be able to see Jenna glowing as radiant as the Madonna with their child growing inside her.

"I don't like this line," Coop said, pointing to the page. "It doesn't sound like my character."

"Read it to me," Shane said reaching for his laptop, which sat open on the burl wood coffee table.

"What's wrong? You're moving funny. Got another headache?"

A life ache. "Yeah. I keep forgetting to call that doctor in Rapid to get him to renew my prescription."

"Oh. Sorry. So, um…page thirty-seven. Midway down. Cooper is talking to his agent, Wiley—love the name, by the way—and he, um, I say, 'So, the deal costs me a little sperm. So what? It's not like I'm using it at the moment. Most of the time it just winds up going down the drain of my shower.'" He looked up. "Can we cut that?"

"Why?"

"Because I don't want my kid to watch this some day and think I, um, masturbated."

Shane blinked. "Those are your words, Cooper. You said them to me when you first talked about answering Libby's ad. I didn't make that up."

"I know, but I'm gonna be a dad, Shane. I have to think like a dad, not some goofy playboy actor."

The pain in Shane's head tripled. "You're going to be an unemployed actor if you don't stop this nitpicking."

"But, Shane, what if it was your kid?"

My kid.

The silence between them grew to a ponderous weight

that finally caught Cooper's attention. He blinked in surprise as if his words had finally caught up with him and tapped him on the shoulder, saying, "Uh, mister, you're an insensitive jerk."

Coop groaned and walked to where Shane was sitting. He put his hand on Shane's shoulder. "Sorry, man. I'll say the line. Just like it's written. You're right. It's dumb to worry about something that might not even happen—especially so far in the future, right?" He set the script on the table and started toward the patio. "Can we take a break? I wanna call Libby and see if she's okay. Can I bring you a beer or anything?"

Shane didn't shake his head for fear of setting off the pain again. "Yeah. A shot of tequila."

He was only half joking. He didn't normally drink in the middle of the day, but the temptation had been growing.

He let his head fall to one side of the soft cushion. He could see Coop outside, on the phone. Smiling that goofy, guy-in-love smile.

What if Coop's right? he suddenly thought. *Maybe I am making too much of something that might not even happen. I could be sterile. Or Jenna might not even want a family. We never talked about it. God, I'm such a self-centered jerk. I didn't even give her a chance to tell me to go to hell.*

When the pressure behind his eyes became too great to bear, he got up and walked to the cabinet in the kitchen where he kept his sparse supply of over-the-counter painkillers.

He might not be able to get rid of the source of these headaches, but he'd do his best not to feel a thing—for a few hours.

"HE'S GORGEOUS, isn't he?" Jenna asked of her two travel mates. Libby was behind the wheel of Rollie's magnificently restored classic Woodie Station Wagon. Her mom was in the passenger seat, and sleeping peacefully in a mammoth dog crate in the rear area was her dog. Not the puppy she'd planned to buy, but the answer to her prayers, nonetheless.

"He's perfect," Libby said, glancing in the rearview mirror. "Can we not talk about him, though? Every time you do I start to cry, and the traffic is picking up."

Jenna tried not to pout. But her friend was right. The eleven-month old Bernese mountain dog that had just set her back enough cash that her father would have been tossing and turning in his grave if he hadn't been cremated, had three paws on the proverbial banana peel when Jenna showed up.

"You cannot kill this beautiful animal," she'd shrieked—honest-to-goodness yelled—at the surprised breeders who had expected her to walk away with a squirming little ball of fluff.

Instead, she'd been drawn to a solitary dog sitting in the sweltering heat beside a bowl of untouched kibble. He'd watched her the whole time she and her mother had walked around the beautiful, clean facility. Libby, who'd never gotten past the puppies and the owner's ten-month baby daughter, hadn't been present when the breeder, Dick Jensen, told Jenna the dog's harrowing story.

"His name is Luca. We can't breed him and we don't feel right selling him," said the man who was a long-haul trucker in his day job. He and his wife, Dianna, had fallen in love with the breed and started raising the animals for sale ten years earlier. This was a hobby they took very seriously. And all of the animals she'd seen were well cared for—even Luca, who didn't display any of the light-hearted charm she'd seen from the breeding pair of adult dogs on the property.

"What's wrong with him?" she'd asked, approaching the pen set under a sprawling oak tree.

"Not a damn thing. He's had all his shots. The vet says he's one-hundred-percent healthy. But…well, it's a long story. I won't bore you."

She hadn't been bored. In fact, midway through the saga she and her mother had looked at each other with tears in their eyes and nodded. They'd both known this dog was the reason they were there.

The change of plan meant a side trip into the city of Bakersfield to a pet-supply store to buy a bigger crate and another stop at Costco for a couple of giant-size bags of dog food. Then they were on the road. Luca settling into the plastic travel container as if he understood completely the reprieve he'd been given.

Now she just had to introduce Luca to Shane and somehow convince the man she loved to give her—and himself—a second chance.

CHAPTER SEVENTEEN

The Jenna Murphy Creative Writing Scholarship will be awarded each semester to the student whose hand-written application displays creativity, scholastic aptitude and strong, individualistic vision.

HE'D CHANGED *written* to *handwritten* knowing Jenna would smile when she read the mission statement of the endowment he was in the process of setting up at their alma mater. He planned to fund the scholarship with the money coming to him from his brother's estate.

Working on this project had saved his sanity this week. For five days straight, he had returned home from twelve hours in the madhouse called the CBS Television Network and gone straight to his computer, turning his attention to something real and positive.

He was so excited about the final results, he decided to invite Jenna, Bess, Libby and Coop to the house for a Saturday afternoon swim party, where he planned to unveil his masterpiece. A fully funded, self-perpetuating scholarship for a deserving student intent on becoming a writer.

The money wasn't in the bank yet, but Shane had talked to the administrator of Adam's will and apparently the

estate was substantial enough that Christina, their stepmother, hadn't challenged a default award that had been a
gift left equally to both sons by their mother. Shane had
never heard about the bequeathal when Adam was alive,
naturally, and he didn't want a single dollar for himself.
But he hoped this gesture would please Jenna.

He'd been tempted to call her a dozen times this week,
but he hadn't. There truly hadn't been time during the day,
and at night he'd channeled his love for her into something
that would outlast them both. He hoped.

Before turning off the computer, he scrolled the SDSU
Web site, smiling at the images of familiar landmarks he
remembered from his three-plus years in school. New
buildings had gone up since he left, he noted.

The other day when he'd been on the phone with the
head of the alumni association, he'd halfway toyed with
the idea of checking into what it would take to finish up
his degree. But the reality was he didn't have time. Not
now. He couldn't make any major changes in his life until
after *Sentinel Passtime*'s run was over.

And at the moment, the show's future looked promising. They'd shot the first pilot on Wednesday after two days
of rehearsals. The studio audience had laughed when they
were supposed to and had warmly embraced Cooper's and
Libby's characters. Another character to get a big ovation
was Aggie the dog lady, played by Jenna's mother. That
had pleased Shane.

This weekend the pilot would be shown to test audiences around the country. This part of the game was a real
crapshoot, but he was confident the show—and Coop's
high-profile mug—would help them score high enough
marks to interest sponsors.

Yesterday, based on the feedback he'd gotten from the studio brass, he'd hired four additional writers to help him produce the rest of the scripts they'd need if the show got the green light. None of the four were as fresh, funny and original has Jenna had been, of course.

There was still a small question of whether or not Morgan, Coop's second ex-wife, would be signed to play Libby's role permanently. The banter between Coop and Morgan had felt real, but a bit too biting at times. Plus, Coop was worried about Libby's feelings. Shane hoped they'd be able to settle the issue today.

He glanced at the clock and let out a sigh. His guests would be here soon. He rose to stroll barefoot toward the lanai.

He planned to serve drinks and tapas by the pool. It was a hot summer day and the sparkling water beckoned invitingly. He couldn't wait to see Jenna in a swimsuit—even though he knew the idea was masochistic and would ruin his sleep for weeks to come. But, apparently, he had an addictive personality that couldn't resist temptation when it was in the same town.

He let out a long, heavy sigh. He did think he was getting better. The hectic pace of life in L.A. helped. He actually could go for several hours without thinking about Jenna, if he set his mind to it.

But his two hours were up and without the scholarship project to distract him he was left with nothing to keep him from getting lost in his memories. If he closed his eyes he could almost conjure up her smell, her laugh. What he couldn't account for was the sound of a dog barking. His nearest neighbor had a Yorkie, but this was a deep, bass timbre that seemed both happy and concerned.

"What the heck?" Did Coop get a dog, he wondered, heading toward the door.

The person standing in his entry wasn't Coop. She was a red-haired beauty wearing a stylish black-and-white sundress with a hot-pink belt. But she wasn't looking at him. Her attention was fixed on the young dog at her side.

"Sit, Luca," she commanded, pushing on the dog's hindquarters while the animal, which had to weigh eighty pounds, tried to lick her face. "Stop that, sweetie. We need to make a good impression."

He tightened his grip on the doorjamb to keep from launching himself forward to sweep her into his arms. He wanted to hold her, kiss her, and apologize for being... well, who he was. Instead, he simply watched her, sensing the second she became aware of his presence.

She glanced up through a part in her shaggy new hairdo. He liked it. When she straightened, he saw that the style made the most of her bright, thick hair. The cut was unapologetically fun and gave the impression of a woman who was secure in her own skin.

"Hi," she said, blowing aside her bangs to smile at him. "We're, um, working on some gaps in his training."

"I see that." The large dog's fluffy black tail swished from side to side with enough force to make the ferns in his ever-perfect landscaping wave.

"Shane Reynard meet Luca." She reached down for one of the dog's giant paws for Shane to shake but the dog wasn't having any of that. He nuzzled her with his broad head then licked her cheek again.

"That's his way of hugging," she explained.

"He's big."

"Yes." She sounded proud. "And only eleven months. Isn't he gorgeous?"

Shane made himself pull his focus from her to the dog. Tricolor. The animal's thick, soft-looking coat was predominantly black with a white chest and snowy streak that ran from his nose to crown. Cinnamon-brown hatch marks above his eyes matched the same color on his legs and paws. The dog seemed to be sizing up Shane as intently.

"He's a Bernese mountain dog, of course."

Of course? "Oh…right. Aggie the dog lady said I looked—"

"No." She stood straight, shoulders back as if delivering a practiced lecture. "Mom made this call long before there was an Aggie. Mom said she could see that you shared certain attributes with the breed, and after doing some research, I agree. Can we come in?" She glanced over her shoulder. "Cooper and Libby and Mom dropped us off so you and Luca could get acquainted without a crowd. Coop said to tell you they'd return in an hour or so with pizzas."

"He did, did he?" Coop knew Shane hated to be manipulated.

His annoyance must have come through in his tone because she held up a small phone. "I can call him to come back if you'd rather not."

"You broke down and bought one?"

"Two, actually. Mom said they're a must in L.A."

She gave him a questioning look that seemed to say, "Are we welcome here or not?" He'd planned to see her, even if he hadn't expected a dog to accompany her. He shouldn't feel this off-kilter. But he did. He felt like a kid meeting his girlfriend's parents for the first time.

"Come in. Is he housebroken?" he joked. What he really wanted to ask was the dog a gift? He hoped to God not.

"Of course. He's very smart. He knows how to sit and shake, but he's so curious and energetic he sometimes has trouble remembering his manners." When she stepped forward, the dog stayed at her heels. He seemed attuned to her, but at the same time appeared interested in all the new sights and smells as they walked through the house.

Shane had bought the place because of the open floor plan. The bedrooms were on the second floor, which could be seen through the Moorish-style arches that added light and texture to the great room. He pointed toward the open doors of the patio. "I think it's nice enough to be outside. The yard is fenced, if you want to let him off his leash."

"Great." She looked around. "Beautiful place. Coop said you decorated it yourself. I can see you in it."

Her tone said that was a compliment, and her smile was so warm and conciliatory he simply had to ask, "Jenna, why are you being so nice? We had an ugly breakup. I left you holding a highly charged emotional bag, and even though I've picked up the phone a dozen times since to call and apologize, I obviously haven't. You should hate me."

She let out a loud sigh that made the dog turn sharply and nuzzle her hand for reassurance—or to give comfort, Shane wasn't sure which. She petted the animal's broad head, then looked at Shane and said, "I did. Hate you. For about twelve minutes. I twisted the back off my favorite turquoise hair clip and threw a couple of shoes. One of them knocked a book off the end table. My book. The one my mother had published. It struck me that there might be a parallel between what your brother did to me and the way you left. So I picked it up and started to read."

He could tell this was important so he led her to a pair of padded teak deck chairs set in the shade of a massive palm tree. She sat across from him. "It was interesting reading. A part of me remembered feeling what the words in those poems expressed, but another part felt like a voyeur. That girl wasn't me. Not anymore. Sure, I felt sorry for her, but I also found myself growing impatient. I wanted to take her by the shoulders and say, 'Bad things happen. Bad people exist in this world. You can't let that define you.'"

"You told me that once. You said it was why you hadn't spoken of the rape to your book-club friends."

She nodded. "They know now. They know everything. They're the reason I'm here. Libby called an emergency meeting of Wine, Women and Words and we hashed out my problems, your problems and most importantly *our* problems."

Shane sat back to put a little more physical distance between them. "Jenna, nothing's changed. There is no us. I'm still me. Bad genes and all."

She bit down on her lip and welcomed the dog between her legs. She hugged him lightly. Shane felt a twinge of jealousy. *Lucky dog.*

"I figured you felt that way or you would have called, but then I met Luca. I want to tell you his story, and I want you to promise to keep an open mind. Okay?"

"I'll try."

Her blazing smile made his heart stop momentarily, and he almost missed what she was saying. "Luca's mother gave birth to five puppies. Three females and two males. Luca and his brother, Chaz."

Luca looked up at the sound of his name and she kissed his shiny black nose. "They're purebreds with a long, illustrious pedigree going back to Switzerland. The breeders are very serious about maintaining a healthy population within the breed and they're meticulous about matching the right stud and bitch."

Her cheeks colored slightly at the use of the word. "Anyway, backstory aside, at eight weeks, Luca and Chaz and their sisters were put up for adoption. The females went right away, and the breeders liked Luca's temperament so well they decided to keep him for breeding. Then the family that bought Chaz brought him back. They said he was too rambunctious for their lifestyle."

"Luca's a big dog. I can see how that could be a problem."

She nodded agreeably. "True, but by nature they're so easygoing and quick to train that their owners usually adore them. The breeder offered to give the people Luca in place of Chaz, but the buyers were spooked. They wanted their money back."

Shane had a feeling they were talking serious bucks, but he didn't ask.

"Within a few days, the breeders understood what the buyers meant. Chaz had gone from normal to aggressive. Chaz wouldn't let Luca eat. He tormented his brother constantly, until poor Luca had to fight back. The veterinarian was called in more than once."

"Am I supposed to see a parallel between Chaz and Luca and my brother and me?"

"I do." She reached out and touched him, but he pulled his hands back and stuck them under his armpits.

"Jenna, this doggie fairy tale isn't going to make me change my mind."

"Fine," she said testily, "but at least have the courtesy to hear the rest of the story. The breeders are compassionate, responsible dog people. They tried showering Chaz with affection. They took him to a dog whisperer. Even medication didn't help. 'Chaz's hardwiring wasn't connected properly,' the husband told me."

Shane shrugged. "So, they put him down."

"I think they wish they had. Instead, while they were away one day, Chaz dug his way out of the kennel and attacked a neighbor's dog. A full-grown chow. The family called 9-1-1. The chow's thick fur probably saved his life, but when the authorities got there, Chaz turned on one of the officers. He left them no choice. They shot him. Eerie parallel, don't you think?"

"Between Adam and some dog? That's a bit of a stretch," he said, but he rubbed his arms to hide the goose-flesh her story had produced.

Her smile was rueful and she shook her head. "Well, maybe…if you're looking for excuses to avoid commitment."

He sat forward, resting his elbows on his knees. He could smell dog—which wasn't a bad smell, he decided—and her perfume. "Is that what you think I'm doing? Or is it possible the writer in you wants to tie up all the loose ends of this story so badly you're seeing a correlation where there isn't one?"

Her back stiffened. "Oh, you big dope. Don't you get it? They did an autopsy of Chaz's body and didn't find anything wrong. Outwardly he was a perfect dog. Nurture-wise, he had the same mother, food, attention and living conditions as his littermates, but he went psycho—just like Adam."

He heaved a sigh. "So you bought this dog to prove to me that I'm okay? What if he suddenly snaps one day and you lose a hand? Or a kid?"

She made a face. "That was the breeders' fear, too. The liability issues were huge, but they were also concerned about passing along defective genes—if such genes exist—to future generations. Better, they figured, to have Luca put down and suggest to the owners of the females that they don't breed their pets."

Shane's stomach turned over. "They obviously didn't kill Luca."

"No. Because I showed up and begged them to sell him to me. I'm not ashamed to admit there were tears. I signed papers agreeing not to sue them and to have Luca fixed. That wasn't a big deal to me. I think most people should have their dogs and cats neutered."

"You saved his life."

She nodded. "Just like you saved mine."

The look he gave her was classic Shane—left eyebrow cocked, lips pulled to the right, the furrows she loved in his brow. Her heart was so filled with love she wanted to jump him right there without warning, but she still had to make him see what she knew without reservation.

"Shane, I didn't buy just any old dog. I bought a Bernese mountain dog. A dog that, by some fluke of nature, has the same history as you." A nervous giggle bubbled up. "Well, not the successful Hollywood producer part, but the bad twin thing…. Come on, Shane. Admit it. You have to see the correlation. I couldn't have made this up."

His severe look softened. "It's a good story, Jenna. But it doesn't change anything."

She made an impatient sound that spooked Luca. He barked one low, cautionary woof, then looked around, ears upright and eyes wide. He was the most beautiful dog she'd ever seen and she'd fallen in love with him the moment she saw him. He was Shane in dog form. She knew it, even if Shane was blind to the fact.

"I can understand why you might choose to be obtuse, Shane, but I've thought about this all week, and here's what I know. The fact Chaz was a bad dog doesn't make Luca any less of a Bernese mountain dog. He's smart and brave and gentle and very sweet. I love him."

She put her arms around the dog's neck and squeezed. Luca responded with unequivocal, tail-whacking affection. Then she looked at Shane. "And I also know that Adam's problems—whether a fluke of nature or product of nurture—do not make you any less of a man. You're smart and brave and loyal, and I love you."

His eyes were filled with emotion but she could tell he meant to push her away again—for her own good. So she launched herself at him, pinning him to the chaise. "I didn't want to have to do this, but I'm going to beg. I'm warning you, there might be tears. It worked for Luca, and I'll be damned if I'm going to let you throw away our chance at happiness because you think you're going to save me from having to suffer the misfortune of growing old with you. Good grief, Shane. Why is that supposed to scare me? I love you. I want you to marry me."

"And have children."

"Possibly."

"Probably. And you should, Jenna. You'd make a great mom."

She kissed him. "I don't know why you'd say that, given my parents, but thanks for the compliment. And I understand completely that you think you're a genetic risk. I don't agree, but I'm prepared to go back to college and study genetics until I prove you wrong."

She saw that that got his attention. "You're going back to school?"

"Yes, I am. My father was a Ph.D. I think I should be able to get a degree or two before I'm too old to reproduce."

"You could apply for the Jenna Murphy scholarship."

She didn't know what he was talking about. She kissed him again then said, sternly, "Quit trying to change the subject. If you don't like my version of this story, we could fly Char out to give you the Lakota medicine man's take on the subject. I'm not sure you'd like the part of you stringing up Adam from a tree…oh, never mind. I need you to answer one question for me."

"What?"

"If I were the one with the evil twin, what would you tell me to do? Become a nun? Get my tubes tied? Run the Mystery Spot…alone…miserable…until they found my cold, dead body in the maze where I tripped over my walker and died of exposure because nobody missed me?"

He shuddered. "Of course not. You deserve a full, rich life with a family and everything."

"I'll have that with you, Shane. You came to the Hills to rescue me from my past. You did that. I'm no longer that shattered young girl afraid of life. I haven't had a nightmare since the first day we started working together. You're my hero, Shane, and I'm not going to let you ruin my happy ending. I won't. Luca and I are here to stay. Get used to it."

His low rumble made her warm from the inside out, but it scared Luca, who barked and pressed closer to her side. Shane petted him. "Hush, boy, it's okay. Everything's fine. No, I take that back. Everything's great."

And Jenna knew without a doubt he was right.

* * * * *

Be sure to pick up the next book in the
SPOTLIGHT ON SENTINEL PASS *miniseries!*
Look for
DADDY BY SURPRISE
by Debra Salonen
coming in January 2009
from Harlequin Superromance.

Turn the page for a sneak preview of
AFTERSHOCK,
a new anthology featuring New York Times
bestselling author Sharon Sala.

Available October 2008.

n✹cturne™

*Dramatic and sensual tales
of paranormal romance.*

Chapter 1

October
New York City

Nicole Masters was sitting cross-legged on her sofa while a cold autumn rain peppered the windows of her fourth-floor apartment. She was poking at the ice cream in her bowl and trying not to be in a mood.

Six weeks ago, a simple trip to her neighborhood pharmacy had turned into a nightmare. She'd walked into the middle of a robbery. She never even saw the man who shot her in the head and left her for dead. She'd survived, but some of her senses had not. She was dealing with short-term memory loss and a tendency to stagger. Even though she'd been told the problems were most likely temporary, she waged a daily battle with depression.

Her parents had been killed in a car wreck when she was

twenty-one. And except for a few friends—and most recently her boyfriend, Dominic Tucci, who lived in the apartment right above hers—she was alone. Her doctor kept reminding her that she should be grateful to be alive, and on one level she knew he was right. But he wasn't living in her shoes.

If she'd been anywhere else but at that pharmacy when the robbery happened, she wouldn't have died twice on the way to the hospital. Instead of being grateful that she'd survived, she couldn't stop thinking of what she'd lost.

But that wasn't the end of her troubles. On top of everything else, something strange was happening inside her head. She'd begun to hear odd things: sounds, not voices—at least, she didn't think it was voices. It was more like the distant noise of rapids—a rush of wind and water inside her head that, when it came, blocked out everything around her. It didn't happen often, but when it did, it was frightening, and it was driving her crazy.

The blank moments, which is what she called them, even had a rhythm. First there came that sound, then a cold sweat, then panic with no reason. Part of her feared it was the beginning of an emotional breakdown. And part of her feared it wasn't—that it was going to turn out to be a permanent souvenir of her resurrection.

Frustrated with herself and the situation as it stood, she upped the sound on the TV remote. But instead of *Wheel of Fortune,* an announcer broke in with a special bulletin.

"This just in. Police are on the scene of a kidnapping that occurred only hours ago at The Dakota. Molly Dane, the six-year-old daughter of one of Hollywood's blockbuster stars, Lyla Dane, was taken by force from the family apartment. At this time they have yet to receive a ransom demand. The house-keeper was seriously injured during the abduction, and is, at the present time, in surgery. Police are hoping to be able to talk to her once she regains consciousness. In the meantime, we are going now to a press conference with Lyla Dane."

Horrified, Nicole stilled as the cameras went live to where the actress was speaking before a bank of microphones. The shock and terror in Lyla Dane's voice were physically painful to watch. But even though Nicole kept upping the volume, the sound continued to fade.

Just when she was beginning to think something was wrong with her set, the broadcast suddenly switched from the Dane press conference to what appeared to be footage of the kidnapping, beginning with footage from inside the apartment.

When the front door suddenly flew back against the wall and four men rushed in, Nicole gasped. Horrified, she quickly realized that this must have been caught on a security camera inside the Dane apartment.

As Nicole continued to watch, a small Asian woman, who she guessed was the maid, rushed forward in an effort to keep them out. When one of the men hit her in the face with his gun, Nicole moaned. The violence was too reminiscent of what she'd lived through. Sick to her stomach, she fisted her hands against her belly, wishing it was over, but unable to tear her gaze away.

When the maid dropped to the carpet, the same man followed with a vicious kick to the little woman's midsection that lifted her off the floor.

"Oh, my God," Nicole said. When blood began to pool beneath the maid's head, she started to cry.

As the tape played on, the four men split up in different directions. The camera caught one running down a long marble hallway, then disappearing into a room. Moments later he reappeared, carrying a little girl, who Nicole assumed was Molly Dane. The child was wearing a pair of red pants and a white turtleneck sweater, and her hair was partially blocking her abductor's face as he carried her down the hall. She was kicking and screaming in his arms, and when he slapped her, it elicited an agonized scream that brought the other three running. Nicole watched in horror as one of them ran up and put his hand over Molly's face. Seconds later, she went limp.

One moment they were in the foyer, then they were gone.

Nicole jumped to her feet, then staggered drunkenly. The bowl of ice cream she'd absentmindedly placed in her lap shattered at her feet, splattering glass and melting ice cream everywhere.

The picture on the screen abruptly switched from the kidnapping to what Nicole assumed was a rerun of Lyla Dane's plea for her daughter's safe return, but she was numb.

Before she could think what to do next, the doorbell rang. Startled by the unexpected sound, she shakily swiped at the tears and took a step forward. She didn't feel the glass shards piercing her feet until she took the second step. At that point, sharp pains shot through her foot. She gasped, then looked down in confusion. Her legs looked as if she'd been running through mud, and she was standing in broken glass and ice cream, while a thin ribbon of blood seeped out from beneath her toes.

"Oh, no," Nicole mumbled, then stifled a second moan of pain.

The doorbell rang again. She shivered, then clutched her head in confusion.

"Just a minute!" she yelled, then tried to sidestep the rest of the debris as she hobbled to the door.

When she looked through the peephole in the door, she didn't know whether to be relieved or regretful.

It was Dominic, and as usual, she was a mess.

Nicole smiled a little self-consciously as she opened the door to let him in. "I just don't know what's happening to me. I think I'm losing my mind."

"Hey, don't talk about my woman like that."

Nicole rode the surge of delight his words brought. "So I'm still your woman?"

Dominic lowered his head.

Their lips met.

The kiss proceeded.

Slowly.

Thoroughly.

* * * * *

Be sure to look for the
AFTERSHOCK *anthology next month,*
as well as other exciting paranormal stories
from Silhouette Nocturne.
Available in October wherever books are sold.

nocturne™

NEW YORK TIMES BESTSELLING AUTHOR

SHARON SALA

JANIS REAMES HUDSON
DEBRA COWAN

AFTERSHOCK

Three women are brought to the brink of death...
only to discover the aftershock of their trauma has
left them with unexpected and unwelcome gifts of
paranormal powers. Now each woman must learn to
accept her newfound abilities while fighting for life,
love and second chances....

Available October wherever books are sold.

SPECIAL EDITION™

BRAVO FAMILY TIES

Tanner Bravo and Crystal Cerise had it bad
for each other, though they couldn't be more
different. Tanner was the type to settle down;
free-spirited Crystal wouldn't hear of it.
Now that Crystal was pregnant, would
Tanner have his way after all?

Look for

HAVING
TANNER BRAVO'S
BABY

by *USA TODAY* bestselling author
CHRISTINE RIMMER

Available in October wherever books are sold.

REQUEST YOUR FREE BOOKS!

2 FREE NOVELS PLUS 2 FREE GIFTS!

HARLEQUIN®
Super Romance®

Exciting, emotional, unexpected!

HARLEQUIN

Super Romance

COMING NEXT MONTH